Gil boiled. Why didn't this kid take the hint and go? Instead, Enko gave Gil a look of pity—as if he thought Gil's anger was childish.

Gil saw red. He clenched his fists. Enko raised a hand. Later, Gil would admit that it had been a defensive gesture, but at that moment, he viewed it as all the provocation he needed. He threw everything he had into a punch he aimed for Enko's jaw.

Enko ducked sideways, deflected Gil's arm and spun him around. Infuriated, Gil lowered his shoulder and tackled Enko hard, knocking him down to the gravel-specked grass. He wanted to get on top and land the missed punch, but Enko flipped him over. Soon Gil was using every wrestling move he had ever learned.

Enko fought tough, attempting to pin Gil, although he never threw a punch. Gil managed to slip through the holds, but he couldn't get a grip on Enko. Gil's legs were scratched and bruised, his arms scraped. Gil knew Enko was receiving the same, but neither boy let up.

Somewhere at the back of his mind, Gil heard the crunch of wheels on gravel. But it wasn't until the siren blasted that the boys jumped apart, panting. A police car stood just twenty feet away, the officer stepping out the driver's side. Gil and Enko scrambled to their feet.

ALSO BY A. C. E. BAUER
No Castles Here
Come Fall

GIL MARSH

A. C. E. Bauer

EMBER

Text copyright © 2012 by A. C. E. Bauer
Cover art copyright © 2012 by Claire Morgan/Trevillion Images

Visit us on the Web! randomhouse.com/teens

Educators and librarians, for a variety of teaching tools,
visit us at RHTeachersLibrarians.com

The Library of Congress has cataloged the hardcover edition of this work as follows:
Bauer, A. C. E.
Gil Marsh / A. C. E. Bauer. — 1st ed.
p. cm.
Summary: High school track star Gil Marsh comes to terms with the loss of his
close friend and teammate, Enko, and his own mortality while on a journey to find
Enko's grave in this modern retelling of the ancient Sumerian tale of Gilgamesh.
ISBN 978-0-375-86933-4 (trade) — ISBN 978-0-375-96933-1 (lib. bdg.) —
ISBN 978-0-375-98311-5 (ebook)
[1. Death—Fiction. 2. Voyages and travels—Fiction. 3. Best friends—Fiction.
4. Friendship—Fiction. 5. Track and field—Fiction.] I. Gilgamesh. II. Title.
PZ7.B3257 Gil 2012 [Fic]—dc23 2011024113

ISBN 978-0-375-87374-4 (pbk.)

Printed in the United States of America

10 9 8 7 6 5 4 3 2 1

First Ember Edition 2013

To the generations of family and friends
who have sat on the porch and loved the view

GIL MARSH

1
Gil Marsh

First day of school. Coach yelled from across the field. "Marsh! Meet our latest recruit."

Gil stopped stretching and jogged over. Coach spoke to a boy dressed in a running tank and shorts. Thick black hair covered the boy's knuckles and arms. It poked out from his chest, his shoulders and neck. It covered his legs. A beast boy, Gil thought.

". . . help you out. He's one of our best runners." Coach turned to Gil. "Marsh, this is Enko Labette. He's from Quebec."

Hmph. Gil wasn't *one* of the cross-country team's best runners. He was *the* best. No one else came close. He had led James E. Uruk High School to Nationals two years in a row.

"Hi," Gil said.

Enko extended his hand in an oddly formal gesture. Gil shook it.

Enko had a powerful grip—a ring on his pinky finger dug in slightly. He smiled, producing a deep dimple in his chin. He was trying hard to impress.

Well, let's see what the beast boy could do.

"You follow me," Gil told him.

He started the warm-up jog just a notch faster than usual. Enko didn't break a sweat.

"Round the back, over the Rock!" Coach yelled to the team. "No clock today. Keep to the running trail. I want it clean and even."

Clock or no, Gil took off, in a sprint now, almost at racing speed.

Enko followed.

They circled around the back of the school to one of the paths along the Green Valley Creek, over the footbridge to cross the water, then up the side of Overhang Rock. The other boys lagged behind.

Overhang Rock stood three hundred feet above town. Made of exposed, weathered red stone, it had a war memorial at the top, erected some ninety years ago by a veterans' group. A running trail wound alongside a road that led to the memorial.

Gil ignored the running trail and chose a hiking path that switchbacked in the other direction, zigzagging at sharp angles around and up the other side of the Rock. At a walk, the trail provided a small challenge. At a run, it required all your concentration to get from one boulder to the next without falling. Gil could do the path in the dark—had done so numerous times. Enko, much to Gil's surprise, took to it as if he could run it blindfolded.

By the time they reached the Memorial, sweat trickled down Gil's back.

"We follow the road down," he said. "Safer that way."

Enko nodded. He wasn't the least bit winded. Who was this kid?

Gil sprinted even faster downhill.

When they returned to the field behind the high school, Coach was waiting for them. "What the hell is the matter with you, Marsh? I said the running trail, not the climbing one!"

Gil leaned forward, hands on his thighs, panting. This had been more of a workout than he had expected. Enko breathed a little harder, too, but wasn't out of breath.

"It's okay, Coach," Enko said. He had this weird French accent. "That was fun."

Fun!

Coach scowled. "Maybe Marsh can learn something from you." He might have said more, but off in the distance two runners trickled onto the field.

"Cool-down walks!" he yelled. "*Everyone,*" he added pointedly to Gil.

When Coach turned to address the other boys, Enko slapped Gil on the shoulder. Gil walked ahead, ignoring the gesture. Beast Boy had just outperformed him. No one had done that before. And Coach had noticed.

2
Beast Boy

At lunch the next day, Gil sat beside Robert Spinozi, as usual. Jennifer Royland walked past with some friends and waved. Gil waved back. Jennifer was the most sought-after girl in school—Gil had been her date last year when she was the junior prom queen and he was a sophomore.

"Boy, you have it easy," Robert said.

"What does that mean?"

"You're popular, girls like you, teachers think you're smart."

"Takes work," Gil said.

And he did put in effort. You needed to be liked to be popular. As team captain, he had made sure the cross-country team volunteered for school and civic activities. And when some teammates stole snacks reserved for the Special Ed room, he made them replace them, plus some. Granted, Gil was tall, blond and a boyish handsome, something that had come to him by luck. Still, he didn't just sit back and wait for good things to happen.

"See the new kid?" Robert asked.

"He runs cross-country," Gil said. Yesterday's humiliation was still fresh in his mind. He lowered his voice. "A beast boy. He's covered in hair."

"Really?" Robert said.

Robert Spinozi was the Grand Central Station for Uruk High's rumors. They all crossed his path, and he sent them out to every far-flung place in the school. Gil knew that Enko would be "Beast Boy" from here on in.

Somehow, the nickname never mattered.

In the shower after practice the next day, LeRoy Brown threw Enko a fine-toothed comb. "For your fur, Beast Boy."

Enko examined the comb. "You know, it's perfect for my arms." He ran the comb over his biceps. "But I'll need something stronger for my legs." He waved the comb at LeRoy. "You sure you don't want to keep it for your chest?"

Laughter all around.

Nothing seemed to faze Enko.

"What's with the pinky ring?" Frank Jones asked during warm-ups.

"My father gave it to me," Enko explained. "It's supposed to bring luck."

No one bothered him about it after that. Besides, kids liked him.

He made fun of his own accent. "At the supermarket, I say 'Excuse me,' and the next thing I know, this older guy asks me what I think about a bottle of wine."

"What'd you say?" LeRoy asked.

"'It's from *Bourgogne*.'" He pronounced it the French way. *Boor-gone-yuh*.

LeRoy appeared impressed.

Enko dropped his voice and grinned. "It says so on the label." He paused. "In English."

He became a rising star. He was a good student and a great athlete. Although stockier than Gil, he had more endurance. His times were faster, too—always a notch ahead.

People paid attention. "Marsh, you stick to Labette," Coach decreed. Boys started asking Enko about his warm-up routine, what he ate, his favorite shoes.

In public, Gil was magnanimous. "The team will be unbeatable," he told Robert, "now that it has both Enko and me." But it bothered him. Until now, he had been first, he had been looked up to. He needed to take corrective action.

Gil had always trained at daybreak. He ran the Rock's hiking trails, leaping boulders and scrambling up steep faces to the top, with its panoramic view of the valley below. He'd whoop at the wind whipping off the cliff's edge, and welcome the rising sun with a bow. He felt alive up there, as if he were in charge of the waking world.

Now he ran the Rock morning and night. He visited the weight room in the afternoons when he didn't have practice. His times improved, and Enko did seem to work harder to stay ahead.

Even so, Jennifer Royland invited Enko, not Gil, to Homecoming.

Robert elbowed Gil when he heard. "What a shame. Now

you have to choose between all those other Uruk girls who are dying to go out with you."

"Except for Amy," Gil said. Amy Kahn was Robert's longtime girlfriend.

Robert shot Gil a warning look. "No, not Amy."

Gil gave him a grin. But Jennifer's choice hurt all the same.

Early one Saturday, Gil stretched in the driveway. A light frost covered the lawn. He wore a pair of gym shorts, a dirty sweatshirt and his shoes. Dawn hadn't quite broken—the sky only hinted at morning. He planned to reach the top of the Rock just as the sun crested the horizon.

He felt loose and limber. The frozen air burned slightly down his throat, but it didn't slow him. He spooked a pair of partridges in one of the clearings near the Creek, and passed a coyote that scooted under some brush, a rabbit hanging from its jaws. Sure-footed, Gil ran to the top of the hill, breathing easy, feeling great, ready to embrace the sun.

He stopped cold when he noticed a figure standing by the war memorial. Enko Labette.

"What are you doing here?" Gil demanded.

Enko looked as surprised at seeing Gil as Gil was at seeing him.

"Wanted to see the sun rise," Enko said.

What kind of an answer was that? This was *Gil's* sunrise. Others might have been up here with him on occasion—some he'd invited, some he hadn't. But Enko? Beast Boy? Did Gil have to share this one private moment of glory with him, too?

"Get out of here."

"Why?" Enko asked.

il sputtered. He couldn't explain. "Because I say so!"

Enko didn't move. He blinked. "Listen—"

"No, you listen. I'm here every day. It's something I do for myself, by myself."

Enko stretched his hands out. "It's a park."

Gil boiled. Why didn't this kid take the hint and go? Instead, Enko gave Gil a look of pity—as if he thought Gil's anger was childish.

Gil saw red. He clenched his fists. Enko raised a hand. Later, Gil would admit that it had been a defensive gesture, but at that moment, he viewed it as all the provocation he needed. He threw everything he had into a punch he aimed for Enko's jaw.

Enko ducked sideways, deflected Gil's arm and spun him around. He crouched slightly, his body taut, his arms bent to his sides, his hands open, ready for whatever Gil planned next. Infuriated, Gil lowered his shoulder and tackled Enko hard, knocking him down to the gravel-specked grass. He wanted to get on top and land the missed punch, but Enko flipped him over. Soon Gil was using every wrestling move he had ever learned.

Enko fought tough, attempting to pin Gil forward and back, although he never threw a punch. Gil managed to slip through the holds, but he couldn't get a grip on Enko. He pushed Enko over, only to be flipped back. His legs were scratched and bruised, his arms scraped where the sleeves had ridden up. Gil knew Enko was receiving the same, but neither boy let up.

Somewhere, at the back of Gil's mind, he heard the crunch

of wheels on gravel. But it wasn't until the siren blasted that the boys jumped apart, panting. A police car stood just twenty feet away, the officer stepping out the driver's side. Gil and Enko scrambled to their feet.

"What's going on?" the officer said.

She was short, at least a head shorter than Gil. But she looked weathered and tough. Gil glanced at Enko, who dusted himself off with deliberate movements.

"Sorry, Officer," Enko said between breaths. "We were practicing."

She lowered her chin, frowning in disbelief.

"Wrestling," Enko said. "It's for . . . tone."

"Up on the Rock?"

Gil could see her eyeing the scrapes and bruises. He felt a tiny trickle behind his ear—blood, he figured. He followed Enko's lead.

"We're on the cross-country team," he said. "We run here every morning."

The officer must have taken note of the running shorts, shoes and dirty sweatshirts.

"You might want to pick softer ground," she said.

Enko grinned—a disarming smile, Gil realized as the officer's face softened.

"We'll remember that," Enko said.

"Is it okay if we finish up?" Gil asked.

The officer nodded.

The boys waved as they jogged down a side path. They ran several switchbacks to a bend hidden by boulders and bushes, and Gil stopped. Enko stopped, too.

Gil turned to Enko, Beast Boy, ready to tell him to stay off his turf from now on. He clenched his fists and stared him down. Or at least, that's what he had planned to do.

"You're one impressive athlete," Enko said.

Gil hadn't expected that. He opened and shut his mouth once, twice, and stared. Seconds ticked away to a minute. Enko's deep-set brown-verging-on-black eyes revealed only calm and patience.

"You're not bad yourself," Gil finally said.

He turned. They jogged down silently, together.

3
Homecoming

Gil would never be able to explain what had happened. It was as if someone had removed a pair of smoked glasses and he could see clearly for the first time.

Enko had never been his enemy. Though he was dark and hairy while Gil was golden and smooth, Enko was also smart, charming, strong, with an edge that Gil liked. From the beginning, he had been game for whatever Gil suggested. He had laughed at himself. He had pushed Gil to improve his performance while acknowledging his strengths. And he had pulled Gil out of trouble not once but twice—with Coach and with the police officer.

When they ran down that morning, Gil knew that he respected Enko. Perhaps he should get to know him.

After that, they began training together. Enko joined Gil and Robert for lunch. Gil's history teacher asked him if he could give Enko some extra help. "He's a little rusty on

American history." And so they began studying together. But more than anything else, they ran. Every morning. Rain or shine. Up to the top of the Rock.

They took State Championships. They were set to beat other states in Regionals.

Robert began to feel left out. "What's with you and Beast Boy? Lovers or something?"

Gil smiled. "We kissed and made up."

Robert laughed, though Gil thought he heard uneasiness in the laughter.

Homecoming rolled around, and Robert suggested that he and Amy split the cost of a limo with Gil and his date. "If we find a third couple, it won't be that much," he added.

"How about Enko?" Gil said.

Robert's eyes narrowed.

Gil gave him a sly smile. "And Jennifer."

Robert shook his head in mock disapproval. "She already made her choice."

"Maybe. But Enko's parents will be out of town that weekend, and he's invited us over after the dance."

"You're a dog, Gil."

Gil grinned, but he had lied to Robert. Gil had no particular interest in Jennifer. She had been a fun date last year, and she made any boy shine. He had invited Lynette Baker to the dance this year, an old friend who was smart and pretty and with whom he knew he'd have fun. Having Enko along simply felt right. Gil couldn't think of a third couple he'd rather spend the evening with.

The night of the dance was electric. Although Uruk lost the

football game to a neighboring town, the cross-country team had clinched the Eastern Division earlier that afternoon—and Gil broke a school record. Everyone was in a celebratory mood.

The music blasted and the emcee called for the homecoming king and queen. "A round of applause, please, as they start us off for the evening."

The king, the football team's quarterback, led the queen, one of the school's best swimmers, to the center of the dance floor.

Robert leaned over to Gil. "You should've been king."

Gil laughed. "Next year."

Enko furrowed a brow. "Why not this year?"

"It's a school tradition," Jennifer explained. "The king and queen are always seniors."

Enko's crooked smile told everyone at the table what he thought about that tradition.

After the royal couple had circled the floor a few times, the emcee announced, "Let's all join them now."

Couples from across the room began flocking around them. Gil's table rose, too. Enko reached out a hand to Jennifer. "Would you care to dance?"

Within a few musical bars, Enko and Jennifer owned the dance floor. Gil and Lynette were good dancers and looked mighty fine on the floor. But Jennifer and Enko were better than good. Enko knew how to show Jennifer off at every turn. As a couple, they were riveting. No one else was worth watching. Gil was impressed.

At the end of the set the emcee called out, "Let's give a hand to our royal couple!"

Kids clapped. Many claps were directed to the king and queen. But even more went to Enko and Jennifer. Enko bowed to Gil and Lynette. Gil bowed in return and swept an arm out to encompass the nominal king and queen, who pretended not to understand what was going on.

The room understood. Whoever might be wearing the crown that evening, Gil was the king, and Enko was his right-hand man. Gil placed a friendly hand on Robert's shoulder. Robert beamed.

The rest of the evening centered on them. Kids watched what they did—when they chose to eat, or decided to dance, or sat out a song. If the homecoming king and queen felt up-staged, they didn't let on. After all, Gil and Enko were the school champions.

The dance ended at midnight. The limo had been rented till two a.m.

"I heard there's a party at Stone Orchards," Gil said.

Everyone at the table was game. A bubble of good humor followed them into the car.

Located in the north of town, the orchards were part working farm, part autumn attraction for the pick-your-own crowds that mobbed the place on weekends for hayrides, pumpkins, apple picking and a corn maze. When the limo pulled into the driveway, all the buildings were dark.

The driver stopped in front of the shuttered snack bar. "Where next?" he asked.

"Let me check it out," Gil said. "It might be in the back."

"I don't want trouble," the man said.

"There won't be trouble," Gil said. "I'm just checking it out."

They spilled out of the car and gathered around picnic tables by the parking lot. The moon was bright, and it felt festive.

"They have an outbuilding this way," Gil said. He pointed around back toward the orchards.

"I'm not walking there in heels," Amy said.

Robert crossed his arms. "My father'll kill me if I damage his tux."

"All right, I'll take a look and be right back," Gil said.

Enko didn't say anything but followed. A dirt footpath led them to signs pointing to the trees for the pick-your-own crowd. Gil ignored them and headed for a row of trees that had been cordoned off.

"I didn't hear about any party," Enko said.

Gil ducked under the rope. "That's 'cause there isn't one."

Enko stood on the other side of the cord. "Then what are we doing here?"

Gil paused. "Haven't you ever wanted to pick apples when no one else was around?"

"Pick apples?" Enko said. "You're kidding, right?"

"When I was little, my mom used to bring me here every year. I'd look forward to it—it was the highlight of our fall. But we were always forced to pick from one or two rows of trees, and I always wanted to come back here and go down the good rows."

Enko stepped back in disgust. "There are five people expecting a party, not some pathetic apple-picking gig."

"And we'll give them one. We'll pick a few apples, tell the guys we didn't find the party, head over to your place and have fun. Just like we planned. It'll only take a couple of minutes."

Enko stood firm. "Don't you have to pay for what you pick?"

Gil huffed, exasperated. "It's only apples."

"Gil—"

"This isn't a big deal. Just keep me company, okay?"

Enko hesitated, then lifted the rope to follow. But the orchard was dark, trees shading the moonlight. Within a few feet he slipped on an apple on the ground, barely avoiding a fall.

"We're in dress shoes!" he growled.

Gil didn't turn around. "Don't be such a wuss. We'll be done in a minute."

He led the way. None of the trees in that area had apples—at least none within easy reach. They had been picked clean.

"Let's try the next row," Gil said.

He stepped between trees to get to it, but no fruits were there, either. They tried a third row, and a fourth.

By this time their pant legs were wet with dew. They had both repeatedly stepped on rotting apples, slid and had to catch themselves. When Enko lost his footing yet again and landed sideways, he rose, dusted himself off, and turned to head back.

"Where are you going?" Gil demanded.

"This stopped being fun a while ago."

"Wait! The next row is full. Look!"

And it was. Trees overflowed with fruit! Gil had no idea what kind of apples these were. He wasn't even sure of their color. But he picked at least half a dozen and handed them to Enko.

"What the hell are you doing?" Enko demanded.

"Getting some more. That way everyone walks away with apples."

Enko looked down at the apples he cradled in his arms. "This is a bad idea."

"Chill. I'm almost done." He held on to even more apples than Enko. "Okay. Let's go."

As they approached the picnic area, a bright beam shone in their direction. It came from a flashlight held by a police officer. The driver stood next to him, backlit by headlights and red and blue flashes. The other kids huddled to the side, Jennifer's arm around Lynette's shoulders, Amy being comforted by Robert.

Crap!

"You. Here!" the officer ordered.

It was too late to drop the apples. Gil and Enko walked deliberately toward the group.

"What's up?" Gil asked.

They deposited the apples on a table.

The officer was an older man who had probably seen more high school pranks in this small town than he cared to remember. He directed the flashlight beam up and down Gil's suit.

"You tell me," the officer said.

Gil knew he had better play this right. He made a show of looking sheepish. He explained that he had hoped to find a party. He had been sure there was an outbuilding back there, but he couldn't find any. "The restroom's closed. And I kind of needed to take a leak. Then I slipped on some apples. . . ."

Enko gave a pained look that said, "Lord knows that kid needs to grow up."

Gil continued the story, feigning embarrassment. They were surrounded by trees and thought they could mitigate everyone's disappointment by bringing them a few apples. "There used to be a scale on the side," he added, pointing to the darkened store. "We were going to leave money in the door."

Enko smiled in agreement.

That did the trick, of course, Enko's smile. The officer didn't exactly soften, but you could tell he was amused.

He took down everyone's name and address, checked the driver's license, then spent time talking on his radio in the police car. No one looked at Gil. Enko's face became blank.

When the officer finally emerged, he handed the driver a slip. "The owner won't press charges. But I have to file a report in case he changes his mind." He tilted his head toward the limo and addressed the kids. "Now get outta here. You're trespassing. And you," he said, addressing Gil and Enko, "leave the apples here."

The driver crushed a cigarette into the pebbles. "They're going home now."

No one argued.

Robert was dropped off with Amy. Lynette and Jennifer were let off at their homes. Gil saw Jennifer give Enko a polite kiss after he walked her to her door. Lynette was less generous. "Next time, Gil, spare us the police, okay?" She shut her door without so much as a wave. At least she had said "next time."

"Who's next?" the driver asked when Gil settled into his seat.

"We go to Enko's," Gil said.

Enko looked at him.

"Unless you'd prefer that I don't come," Gil added.

Enko shrugged. "My mother left me food for an army."

They peeled off their jackets at the front door. Enko wrinkled his nose. "We really stink."

They did—a foul combination of sweat mingled with rotting apples and something nastier that one or both of them must have picked up under their shoes.

"You can use the downstairs shower," Enko said. "I'll leave you an extra pair of sweats on my bed."

Gil had just finished dressing in Enko's room when Enko emerged from the adjoining bathroom, toweling his head. Enko reminded Gil of one of those athletes on Greek urns he had seen during a field trip to a museum. Enko's body was perfectly sculpted. His powerful legs, flat stomach, broad chest and strong arms radiated vigor. And something animal about him added to his attractiveness. Gil understood why Jennifer had asked Enko for the date.

And then, out of embarrassment, or nervousness about

the police encounter, or fatigue from a long and eventful day, or just plain stupidity, Gil couldn't help himself. He giggled.

Enko peeked out from under his towel. "What's the joke?"

Gil had no explanation, so he said the first thing that popped into his head. "How did you ever get so furry?"

Enko didn't smile as he usually did when someone mentioned his hair. "It's the way I am." He pursed his lips, turned his back and opened a drawer.

Gil immediately wished he could take back the words. He had hurt Enko.

This wasn't the first time Gil had said something he wished he hadn't. But this might have been the first time he felt the pain he had inflicted. Enko was beautiful. Yet kids made fun of his hair, as if it mattered.

Gil had, too, on that first day. . . .

How could he have been such an idiot? He took a step forward. "I'm sorry."

Enko didn't turn. He searched the clothes in his drawer with violence. "No, no. Don't be. Now I know what you think."

"Enko—"

Enko's shoulders folded, his head bowed. His voice was harsh. "Not everyone, Gil Marsh, is born smooth and pretty." He turned around, holding a shirt. "Not everyone smiles and then is told by everyone around how clever he is."

He pulled the long-sleeve shirt over his head. He grabbed pants from the drawer and stepped into them as if he couldn't get into them fast enough. He pushed past Gil and headed for the stairs.

Gil had to fix this.

He found Enko in the kitchen, lit by the open refrigerator. Gil stopped in the doorway. Enko grabbed a can of soda and shut the fridge door quietly. Neither boy turned on the room light.

"You don't have a clue, do you?" Enko said.

"I—"

Enko interrupted. "I'm here on my parents' visa." He remained quiet and deliberate, focused on the can, never once looking in Gil's direction. "I get in trouble with the law, and they can kick me out. Just like that." He snapped his fingers. "And now my name is on a police report sitting in the Green Valley Police Department."

"The officer said the owner won't prosecute."

"Let's hope he's right." Enko popped the can and took a long drink.

Gil sagged against the doorframe. He *was* exhausted. He put a hand on his forehead and shut his eyes. Damn it, why hadn't he done any thinking?

Enko walked past him on his way to the stairs.

"I'm going to bed," he said. "There's a couple of air mattresses and sleeping bags in the basement if you decide to stay."

4
Antoine and Clotilde

By Monday morning, everyone in school had heard about the incident at Stone Orchards. Robert, rumormonger that he was, treated it as a great joke. The story went around the Internet social networks a few times, never hurting Gil's and Enko's status. Gil did get some ribbing at practice about whether he needed to pee by the side of the school, but he laughed with the other boys. Someone also left a bag of apples on top of his locker—he shared those with the team. By Wednesday, it was all but forgotten.

The chill between Enko and Gil thawed more slowly.

Nationals were next week, and Coach had them on a full schedule. On Thursday it rained, and Coach restricted them to the track. "No point spraining an ankle today." By the time they finished, everyone was soaked. "Hot showers," Coach said. "I want to see steam everywhere."

The disaster struck in the locker room. Gil slipped as he

was dressing. A random puddle, guys jostling, who knew why it happened. When Gil got up, his leg shot out just as he put his full weight on it. His head smashed against the bench.

He woke to Enko calling, "Gil! Gil!"

"What . . . ?" Gil asked.

He tried to stand but Coach wouldn't let him.

"You stay put, Marsh."

An ambulance arrived, and they strapped Gil in. He tried to stop them.

"I'm okay." He flexed his arms and legs. "See. Everything works."

"We've got to check for a concussion," the attendant told him.

Coach followed the ambulance and agreed to take Enko along. Gil's mother, who had been reached at her office, met them in the emergency room. Coach took her aside to explain what had occurred, while Enko kept Gil company. A couple of ambulances pulled in, filled with trauma victims from a car crash. Gil's X-rays took lower priority and they had to wait.

Gil sat on a gurney. "What a waste of time," he grumbled. "I feel fine!"

"Coach has to follow procedures," Enko said.

A half hour passed, and still they waited.

"There's nothing wrong with me," Gil said. "Why don't we just leave?"

Coach and Mom exchanged glances.

"You were out for several seconds, Marsh," Coach said. "I can't let you run unless the doctors clear you."

What?

"But Nationals are Saturday! We leave tomorrow!"

Coach shook his head. "It's the rules, Gil."

A nurse brought a bunch of forms for Gil's mom to complete. Coach sat with her, filling in some of the details.

Gil felt anger rising. He was going to be sidelined because he slipped in the locker room! He was in the best running shape of his entire life—this season's times were his fastest ever. This just couldn't be happening. He punched the gurney, hard.

He felt a hand on his arm. Enko's.

"Did I ever tell you the legend of the ring?"

Gil scowled. "Which ring?"

Enko sat next to him, took off the ring from his pinky finger and began twisting it. It twinkled under the light. At first glance, the stone looked black, but as some of the light shone through it, Gil saw red, like dark blood.

"Your father gave it to you, right?" Gil said.

"It's a family heirloom."

Enko handed it to Gil, who noticed black streaks in the silver band.

Enko continued. "The story is that it was made in northern *Québec* by an immortal man." He pronounced it *Kay-bek*, the French way.

"Immortal man?" Gil asked.

Enko nodded. "A boy had the immortal man make it for a girl he loved. But she died, and then the boy died, too. It's all very romantic."

Gil didn't think so.

"But still, the ring brings luck," Enko said.

Gil returned it to Enko. "Maybe that's why I smacked my head instead of you."

Enko laughed. "Maybe. The whole story is cool, though, even if it's sad."

"Okay," Gil said. "Go ahead. Tell me. It's not like I'm going anywhere."

More than a hundred and thirty years ago, a settlement of rough farms and a few small businesses subsisted along the Red River, about a hundred miles north of Montreal, many days' journey from the city. There, five-year-old Antoine Larivière fell in love with Clotilde Charette the moment he set eyes on her. She was only four, but her golden ringlets fascinated him. They bounced as she followed her mother out of church. And when the sun reflected off them, he thought she must be an angel.

As Clotilde grew, she gathered the curls into braids and buns and stuffed them under caps. But Antoine always managed to see the small ones that escaped to the sides of her forehead. He noticed her clear blue eyes that matched the summer sky, and her teeth as bright as a first snow.

Clotilde, for her part, thought Antoine a nice-enough boy. Their fathers were good friends, and Antoine often came when M. Larivière visited. Her mother, pious to a fault, approved of M. Larivière, since he was a regular at mass—more regular than her sometimes-wayward husband.

When Antoine turned fifteen, he asked Clotilde to marry him.

Mme. Charette objected. "At fourteen, she is barely a woman."

M. Charette scratched his large belly. "Yes. But they can be engaged."

Antoine was M. Larivière's oldest son and likeliest to inherit his father's store. A sound business, M. Charette assessed, and a place that wouldn't be too hard on his gentle daughter.

Mme. Charette sniffed her disapproval. "He is a gangly, soft boy. He spends his time reading books!"

Reading anything other than the Bible, and that only on Sundays, was a waste of time, as far as Mme. Charette was concerned. Unless, of course, you were studying to become a priest, may the *bon Dieu* bless those with the calling. But the young Antoine was not cut out to be a priest, she could tell.

"Knowing to read is useful in commerce," her husband said.

Mme. Charette allowed that, and permitted the boy to visit Clotilde on Thursday evenings. But Antoine needed to win over Mme. Charette.

He consulted with his father. "How can I get Mme. Charette to take me seriously?"

M. Larivière thought for a moment. "She has a soft spot for jewelry, not that she would ever admit it. But she's proud of the few baubles she wears to church."

Antoine had no money to buy a gift, but he remembered the family garnet, a red, almost black stone M. Larivière found at the bottom of his father's hunting satchel. Story was that Antoine's grandfather had gotten it from a *voyageur* in exchange for some good tobacco. The stone was perfectly round, a little flat, with a large number of tiny facets. M. Larivière kept it in a cabinet, taking it out once every decade or so to be admired. Useless, really.

M. Larivière agreed it could be used. "But it will need to be set."

They decided to ask the local blacksmith. An immortal man. No one knew where he came from. He had been around since the Indians and, it was said, had learned their secret potions and tricks. He was renowned as a healer and crafty with his tools. They brought him an old silver spoon with a twisted handle and misshapen bowl. Whatever wasn't used for the ring would be payment for his work.

The ring the blacksmith created enchanted Clotilde, and her mother even more. Mme. Charette never took her eyes off the garnet.

"A very generous gift," she said.

Mme. Charette stored it with her own few pieces, promising Clotilde that she could wear it on special occasions.

The wedding was scheduled for that fall, after the harvest season.

It never took place.

A few weeks after receiving her gift, Clotilde cut her thumb deeply while helping her mother in the kitchen. Her mother wrapped a washing rag around the wound, and later that night changed the old rag for a clean one. They replaced it again the next day, but the wound festered. In another day or so, the infection spread.

M. Charette wanted to call the immortal man because everyone knew that he could cheat death. He had saved babies with fevers, sewn up innumerable cuts, and set countless bones.

Mme. Charette wouldn't hear of it. "Not that heathen! The village has a good Catholic doctor now. Call him."

But the doctor had been called away to a difficult birth and didn't arrive until the following afternoon. Clotilde lay feverish in bed. She pleaded with her mother to see the ring, but Mme. Charette refused.

"Don't be foolish. You need rest."

The doctor decided to amputate Clotilde's arm, but it was too late. She died the following morning.

Mme. Charette railed against fate, God and the Devil. "You took her from me."

She thought of Clotilde's last few words, begging to see the ring. "Cursed thing."

She sent the ring back to Antoine's family, never to see it again.

The attendant finally arrived to roll Gil to X-rays.

"Wait," Gil said. He turned to Enko. "You have to tell me what happened to Antoine."

"He was inconsolable," Enko said. "He died the following spring."

"So why do you think the ring brings luck?"

"Our family made its fortune soon after getting it."

Gil crumpled his chin. "That was some sad story."

"Many of the *Québec* legends are," Enko said.

"Let's go, son," the attendant said.

5
Inseparable

The results came back positive. Gil had suffered a minor concussion. The hospital admitted him overnight for observation. Not only was he barred from the competition, but he couldn't accompany the team on the bus.

"Too much jostling," the doctor explained.

Gil wanted to break something. "It's Nationals!" he yelled. "We were all set to win!"

"We'll win, Gil," Enko said. "I promise."

Gil grabbed him by the arm. "Wear my number. At least my number will run. And you're as good as me—better even."

Enko gave Coach a questioning look.

"Sure," Coach said. "Enko can wear your number."

"I'll text you," Enko said, "as soon as we finish."

Gil hugged Enko then—a powerful hug, as if he could transfer all of his strength to his friend. Enko hesitated, but only for a second. He hugged fiercely back.

Mom arranged to work from home on Friday, to keep watch over Gil. He sent an unending stream of text messages to Enko, demanding to know every step of his travels. Enko texted back, giving details and passing on the occasional team joke.

That night Coach called lights-out at eleven.

Bedtime, Enko texted.

I'll dream of U, Gil texted back.

Winning?

The champion

No sweat

Promise?

LOL. OK. Some sweat. But I'll win

Gil wished there were some way he could transfer all of his pent-up energy to Enko, give him some extra boost and be part of the meet as well.

I'm w/U, he texted.

Yes, Enko texted back, *U R*

The meet began early on Saturday. It'd be over by mid-morning. Gil waited anxiously by his phone. He tried to distract himself by surfing the Internet, but nothing caught his interest. He couldn't focus on any video games. And the morning cartoons were just too silly. All he could think of was Enko running—his easy gait, the look of relaxed concentration he always had, the way he breathed, the swing of his arms.

The phone's ring caught him by surprise. The text was from Enko!

#1!

Gil's whoop brought his mother over in a hurry.

"Enko won Nationals," Gil said.

Mom grinned. "That's great!"

When the bus returned late Saturday evening, Gil was there, along with all the other cheering family and friends. He threw an arm over Enko's shoulders as soon as he stepped off the bus.

"You are awesome!" Gil said.

Enko looked just a little worried. "You sure . . . ?"

Enko's parents were pushing through the crowd. Gil had only a few more seconds.

"You deserved to win," Gil said. "I'm glad you did."

At that moment, Enko's mother swooped in and folded Enko into a huge hug. His father snapped pictures. Gil stood to the side and beamed.

Yeah, Gil realized, he was glad. Truly, honestly, no qualms about it, glad. He was disappointed that he couldn't have been there—but Enko winning was the very next best thing to being there. And Gil wanted to celebrate his victory wholeheartedly.

If Gil and Enko had been close before, they were now insepa-rable. That Thanksgiving, Enko's family joined Gil's for dinner.

"This is so much fun," Enko's mother said. "Thanksgiving in *Québec* is much earlier in the season and less elaborate."

Over too much food and lots of wine, Enko's parents talked about their move to Connecticut. His father had been offered the opportunity to transfer.

"We thought it would be good for Enko to get some schooling in English, too," his mother added.

"It is the international language of commerce," his father said.

Enko mouthed the words as his father pronounced them, obviously having heard this line a few times too often.

His father gave him a mock slap on the side of his head. "You make fun of me, but it's true."

"Until Mandarin takes over," Gil's father said.

They all laughed.

Gil turned to Enko as they sat on the couch to watch the football game. "Don't they have English schools in Quebec?"

"Sure," Enko said, "but because of the language laws, I couldn't go to them."

Enko explained that in Quebec, only a limited number of kids were permitted to attend publicly funded English schools. He didn't qualify. So if his parents wanted him to receive schooling in English, they either had to pay tuition at an expensive private school or move somewhere else.

"You really didn't have a choice?" Gil asked.

Enko shook his head. "But then, if I did, I wouldn't be here."

The smile he shot Gil warmed him.

Gil invited Enko along for a ski trip New Year's weekend. They drove up to a condo in Vermont that his parents had rented. Enko was almost as good a skier as he was a runner.

"The slopes were half an hour from our house," Enko said. "My parents taught me as soon as I could walk."

In February, Enko invited Gil to come with him to Quebec City.

"The Winter Carnival—it's unbelievable," he said. "Ice sculptures. Slides. Parades. The greatest time in the world."

But Gil's parents had booked a family trip to the Caribbean.

"We'll get together when we're both back," Gil said.

Gil caught something nasty on the plane ride home. It started as a cough that winded him halfway up the Rock his first run back. Enko convinced him that they should turn around. Gil protested. Enko wrapped an arm around him.

"Don't be a fool. I want you strong."

Gil spent the next week in bed fighting bronchitis. Enko visited him every day.

"Don't worry. I'm keeping the paths clear for you."

Somehow that helped Gil improve. But when, a week later, he felt strong enough to run again, Enko was coughing.

"Damn it, Enko. I gave this to you."

Enko smiled and punched him in the arm. "I'm giving it back."

He didn't give it back. But he didn't get better, either. After a week of coughing, Enko's parents had him get a chest X-ray. He was diagnosed with pneumonia.

"They think I caught it in *Québec*." Enko tried to reassure Gil. "A few weeks' rest and I'll be as good as new."

And after a few weeks, the pneumonia did heal, but somehow, he never got better.

"I need more time at Overhang Rock," he said.

But he didn't have the energy to run up the Rock—even

walking it tired him. He was back in bed with a combination ear and throat infection. And a new bout of bronchitis. By late March they had diagnosed his ailment—aggressive leukemia.

There was no time to process the news. Enko was hospitalized and the treatments started immediately. When Gil visited him, he had to dress in a sterilized jumpsuit, mask, hat and gloves. Enko stayed in a special pressurized room that didn't allow any unfiltered air in from the rest of the hospital.

"Gil!" Enko seemed so happy to see him.

Every hair on Enko's body had fallen out. It made him look naked, more naked somehow than Gil had ever seen him before.

"What've you been up to?" Gil asked.

"Watching TV. Reading an ebook. Catching up on stuff online. And sleeping."

Gil sat on the chair next to Enko's bed. "They let me bring in a pack of cards. Freshly sterilized. Want to play poker?"

Enko's mischievous glance, so familiar to Gil, came from exhausted eyes. "I hope you've brought money to lose."

But Enko only lasted a few rounds. He rested his head on the pillows that propped him up, tired out by the effort it took to hold the cards and play. Gil's chest pinched. It wasn't right!

A nurse came in to check on Enko's vital signs and adjust one of the drips attached to his arm. "This boy's a trooper," she told Gil.

Gil nodded, not sure how to respond. When the nurse left them to fetch a new IV bag, Enko grabbed Gil's wrist with a bony, powerful grip.

"Hold me," he said. "Please."

"But I'm carrying germs. You're immunosuppressed. I could kill you."

Enko's eyes filled with tears. "What's the point of living, Gil, if people can only shove needles into me?"

Gil wrapped Enko in his arms and held him, for as long as he could. He didn't let go when the nurse returned. He kept his eyes shut, squeezing away the wetness under his lids, feeling every ragged breath in Enko's body.

Gil visited every day the hospital allowed him. Even when Enko was too weak to stay alert, Gil sat next to him, staring at his ravaged body, memorizing the line of his nose and brow, hoping to catch a glimpse of his dark eyes.

They stopped the chemo cycles after four weeks.

"It wasn't working," Enko said. "If I'm going to die, I want to do it away from here."

His family contacted the local hospice, and Enko moved back home to a room downstairs. Some of his hair grew back.

"A miracle." He laughed. "It's not supposed to happen for months. I guess some things are too strong even for the chemicals."

Gil held his hand, cradled his head, drove him once to the top of Overhang Rock. Gil attended school only to stay out of trouble. Every other waking moment was spent with Enko. A week before he died, Enko gave him the ring.

"I can't take this," Gil said. "It's a family heirloom."

But Enko insisted. He smiled—that smile that could still disarm. "I want it to be yours. You're family now."

Gil didn't speak, afraid words might choke him. He took Enko's hand in his. When Enko's mother came in, Enko had fallen asleep, Gil still holding his hand. She saw the ring on his finger.

"*Le grenat*," she said, and nodded. "Enko loves you very much."

Gil stared down, still unsure whether he should keep this treasure.

"Are you sure you don't want me to return it?" he asked.

She shook her head, her shoulders bowed. "It belonged to Enko. It was his to keep or give. He chose you to have it."

Gil didn't reply.

6
Death's cheat

When the call arrived that Enko had died in the night, Gil did not believe his mother.

"You misunderstood," he said. "His mom's accent . . ."

"I'm sorry, Gil. But I didn't misunderstand. Angine was very clear."

"No. I'm going to call—"

His mother put her hand on the phone.

"Listen to me, Gil. Enko is dead. His parents are overwhelmed. They have arrangements to make. Family to call." She was pleading, Gil realized. Crying even. "Please, honey. It's hard. But he is dead."

"NO!"

He went to his room and put on his sweats and shoes. He ran to Enko's house—and there he saw the hearse. The door to Enko's house was open.

No!

He turned away and ran faster, heading north. He made it all the way to Stone Orchards, where he had been such an idiot at Homecoming. Winded, he looped around. By the time he returned home, he was so tired, he almost collapsed.

At dinner he learned that they had shipped Enko's body back to Quebec—to a family plot in the Montreal area.

"When's the funeral?" Gil asked.

"In a week," his mother said.

"We can book a room now."

His parents exchanged glances.

"It's hundreds of miles north," his dad said.

"And we can't take the time off now," his mom added.

Gil hadn't touched his meal. Food repulsed him.

"Then I'll go alone," he said.

"No," his father said. "You've missed enough school."

"I'll miss the funeral!"

His mother's tone was kind—Gil could hear it even if he would not accept it. "The school will hold a memorial service in a couple of weeks. We'll visit his grave this summer."

"A memorial service!" Gil pushed his plate away, making a glass tip over.

His mother jumped up to mop the mess. His father scowled.

"No one at school knew him," Gil said. "No one! Not like me."

"Don't be an idiot," his father said. "The school will—"

"The school will not do anything!" Gil said. "You don't understand, do you?"

He stood. His mother stepped back. His father rose as well.

"I need to say goodbye. For real. To him. Even if he's stuck inside a box! He was my best friend. He was everything—"

"That's enough," his father said.

His mother reached out. "Everyone is grieving, Gil. His parents' hearts are broken. Their home was there. It's where he belongs."

Gil didn't give up. "Then let me go!"

But his parents wouldn't.

"This summer," they said.

"NO!" he screamed.

He ran back to his room and threw himself onto his bed, where he rolled into his comforter. He tightened it around himself, as if the cocoon he created might keep the world at bay. Enko couldn't be gone. Gone from life. It wasn't possible!

At the memorial service he sat in the back row. The principal, a few teachers, several members of the team, Jennifer Royland, all spoke about Enko in glowing terms. There wasn't a dry eye in the auditorium—except for Gil's. He had refused to speak. These were empty gestures. No one knew Enko the way he had. No one felt the loss the way he did.

He began skipping school entirely. He was called in to the school's main office, his parents dragging him along.

"You have always been an excellent student," the principal said. "We know you lost your best friend, but you still have to attend school."

The guidance counselor recommended a psychologist. Gil went to sessions because his mother drove him there and didn't leave. He never said a word.

He stopped showering. Stopped cutting his hair. A ragged beard grew in around his chin. If there were a cream that would have made his hair grow faster on his skin, he would have bought it. Everywhere he went he remembered Enko.

Here they had studied. Here they had laughed. Here they had run.

Although he attended the last few weeks of school, his father driving him there, his mother bringing him home, he spent his days alone.

Robert tried to reach out.

"I'm thinking of switching to track next year," he said. "Maybe we could run together."

Gil didn't even acknowledge him.

He shied away from everyone, and in return, everyone shied away from him. He passed his classes—barely, thanks to his stellar grades earlier in the year. Come June, he packed his duffel bag and demanded, "So, when are we going to Quebec?"

But his mother's interior design firm was in the middle of three major renovations.

"Clients expect me around," she said. "I'll get a break soon, I'm sure."

His father's company was in the middle of an important deal. "We close in July. After that, I promise."

But July came, and neither could see traveling north.

"Maybe later in the fall," his mother said. "We'll take you out of school. The whole family could use a break."

When the course schedule arrived for his senior year,

something snapped. There on the printout, in bold letters, was the afternoon slot reserved for practices.

Cross-country

Gil was not going to return to school. If no one took him north, he'd take himself. He could no longer bear being in Green Valley, where every place hurt him. He had to find Enko, whether anyone helped him or not.

7
Flight

Gil began by running again.

"I talked to Coach," he said. "He says I need to get back into the saddle."

His father nodded, approving. Pleased, too, that Gil had resumed showering and shaving.

"The Berkshire trip is in three weeks," Gil added.

Every year, Coach organized a team trip to the Berkshire Mountains for the last week of summer vacation. He worked out a deal with a small college to lease a floor in a dorm and to allow team members to use the athletic facilities. They would arrive on Tuesday and leave after lunch on Friday. There, they would run the hilly terrain around campus, take advantage of the exercise equipment and, in their free time, have fun.

"I'm glad you're going," Mom said. "A change of air will be good for you."

Gil wasn't going, at least not on the organized trip. He had never talked to Coach. He wouldn't board the team bus. The Berkshire trip was his cover to escape Green Valley.

Gil forged forms, using last year's as models. He had his mom take him for a sports physical at the family doctor, as she did every year. He saved every penny he could, hiding the cash with his passport. He used the library computer rather than the one at home to track down youth hostels in Montreal so that his parents wouldn't find any record of his searches. His phone had a GPS keyed into his parents' phones, so they'd know where he was. He allowed the battery to drain. Two days before his departure, he announced that it was dead.

"I was going to upgrade anyway," his father told him. "A new phone will arrive in a few days."

"I may have an old one that still works," his mom said. "It's only good for calls and texts. But you can bring it with you."

At least this one didn't have a GPS. He stuffed it at the bottom of his duffel, determined not to use it.

The night before his departure, he told his parents goodbye. "I'm being picked up at five a.m."

"Run well, honey," his mother said. "And have fun." He allowed her to kiss him on the cheek.

Gil tiptoed out at four. He caught a train into the city and a bus north.

Although he was somewhat anxious at first, the ride proved uneventful. No one asked him why he was on a bus by himself, heading north. It had been weeks since Gil had

had time to himself, to think about something other than his plans. Finally, he was on his way to Enko's birthplace. To where he was buried. To say goodbye.

He pushed these last thoughts aside. He needed to hold it together. There were still hundreds of miles to travel, a border to cross, people to deal with before he reached his destination.

Gil ate a sandwich he had packed for lunch, and took a brisk walk when the bus stopped for forty-five minutes at a diner outside of Albany. They traveled farther north, and he watched the Adirondacks rise around him, then dwindle and turn into rolling ground in the Lake Champlain Valley. As the distance grew between him and home, a feeling of lightness grew as well. Yes, he had hard things to do. But away from Green Valley he could be himself, without worrying about what people knew of his past. It gave him a sense of freedom. He was in charge of himself, truly, for the first time.

At the border, the Canadian customs officer was all business.

"Passport?" she asked from across the counter.

Gil handed her the small, three-year-old blue booklet with the photo where he still looked like a little kid.

She flipped the pages and punched something into the computer.

"Traveling alone?"

"Yes."

At seventeen, he was still a minor, so the question was a natural one—one he had expected. He had rehearsed a whole story about visiting a cousin who was meeting him at the bus station. But she didn't ask.

"Destination?"

"Montreal."

"For how long?"

"Two weeks," he said.

He hadn't decided how long he planned to stay. But that answer would have gotten him in trouble, and you didn't ever want to get in trouble with the border police.

"Are you bringing any presents with you?"

The ring on his left hand felt heavy. Gil shook his head.

"Have a nice stay," the officer said.

The older woman behind him stepped up to the counter, her wallet in hand, blue passport on top of it. Gil returned to the bus. He noticed another customs officer leading a dog away from the baggage compartment.

Gil straightened. He didn't like this feeling of being inspected, having every move watched. He knew the customs officials were just doing their job—and they had been polite and professional. But Gil didn't breathe easy until the bus pulled away from the border station.

"*Bienvenu au Québec,*" a sign announced.

He glanced back through the window. No one was following. No alarm had been raised. He had left Connecticut behind.

He corrected himself. He had left the United States behind.

He settled back into his seat. He had done it! If only Enko were there to celebrate with him. He'd have laughed at all the steps Gil had taken to pull this off.

Gil took a deep breath and held it for a few seconds. He exhaled. Time to concentrate on his itinerary.

They were to arrive in Montreal in the early evening. He had packed enough food for tonight, and tomorrow he'd track down Enko's grave. But what then? He had never really gotten past that thought. He couldn't return home. It was too painful. His one goal was to find Enko. But a grave . . . That was just a piece of dirt with Enko, dead, buried under it. That would be painful, too. He wanted more than that. He wanted Enko.

He stared out the window, watching the flat farmland pass by. Without thinking, he fingered the garnet on his finger.

The ring.

An immortal man had made this ring. He had cheated death. Enko had told him so. Maybe he'd know how to bring Enko back!

Yes.

He'd track the man down. But where?

Gil thought back to the story Enko had told him. It had taken place in an old farming village, about a hundred miles north of Montreal. That's what the legend said. North. That was where Gil needed to go.

He shut his eyes.

North.

He had a goal.

8
Apropoulis

The night had been difficult.

Gil had planned to sleep on Mount Royal, in the center of the city, just as he had on Overhang Rock numerous times. On the Rock all he needed was a blanket. He knew the crevices, the bushes, the trees, all the shelters he could use—protection from the morning dew and stray dogs. He had brought Jennifer Royland there after the Junior Prom. He had camped there with Enko, also. But Gil shut down that memory.

Mount Royal wasn't anything like Overhang Rock.

A park covered most of it, with a road, paved paths, parking lots, trails, benches, park buildings and a huge, lit-up cross right at the top. Gil had aimed for the cross, thinking it would be a safe place to spend the night.

Stupid.

The area was crawling with lovers and bums. He interrupted two men under one bush, a reeking drunk in a ditch and what he thought was a prostitute and her john behind some trees. A mounted police officer patrolled the main path. Gil reached a large overlook with a glittering view of the St. Lawrence River and decided to scramble down. A row of buildings abutted the last big stand of trees below. He aimed for an apartment building surrounded by shrubbery and found a spot to curl up in along its side.

He slid into his sleeping bag and tucked his duffel under his head. Hiding in the city was going to be harder than he thought. He had intended to camp in the city's parks while the weather was good, saving what money he had for hostels when the need arose. Who knew there'd be so many people?

Sirens howled. Trucks rumbled. The occasional pedestrian walked by. He slept fitfully. He woke to a cat hissing at him.

Gil hissed back, and the orange cat ran away.

The sky still sported its morning grays—barely light. He brushed dirt off the bags. Where to?

He needed to find Enko's grave—track down the cemetery and the plot. Then he'd head north. That was where he'd find the immortal man. But to get to the cemetery, and then to head north, he'd need transportation.

He checked the money pouch he kept hidden in his shirt—after the train and bus tickets, he had a little more than two hundred and fifty American dollars. His first priority, he realized, was to exchange it for Canadian currency. Making purchases with American dollars was only going to draw attention to himself.

He thought back to the last time he had visited Canada—it had been several years ago, with his parents. They had stayed at a resort that accepted U.S. bills at a premium. But his parents had used the ATM.

"It's so much easier," Mom had said.

Gil had misunderstood at first. "You have a Canadian bank account?"

"No," Dad explained. "But banks will exchange cash for you. And Canadian ATMs will do the exchange straight from our U.S. accounts."

Well. The bank card his parents had given him wasn't an option. It was keyed to their accounts. They'd be able to track him down through the bank—Dad routinely checked their balances online, and the locations of withdrawals were always listed. Gil couldn't risk it. But exchanging his cash at a bank would work.

He glanced at the sky. What time was it? He pulled his mom's old cell phone from the duffel and turned it on. Five-fifteen. No bank was open at this hour. The icon for messages flashed. For a split second he forgot and thought Enko had texted him. He shook his head. Stupid. He must be more tired than he realized. But who had called him? He clicked through.

Good luck @ training. I'll pick you up Fri pm. Love Mom

Of course. Only his parents knew this number. He turned off the phone. Mom wasn't expecting a response. But the message reminded him: he had three days before they discovered he had disappeared. He'd better get himself organized.

A gray tabby spat at him. A black-and-white tom followed her. All these cats! Where did they come from?

Gil scratched himself. He should get out of here anyway, before people noticed him. He dug out his comb and flattened his blond mop. There wasn't much he could do about the stubble around his chin—not until he found a restroom. He fished out his spare jeans and a clean tee, checked to make sure no one could see him and quickly changed into them.

When he stepped out from behind the bushes, he thought he looked okay—a bit rumpled, but no more than any other teenager. He immediately realized why there were so many cats.

The bushes abutted an alley that separated a row of apartments at the edge of the mountain and a row of commercial buildings facing another street. At the rear of one of the buildings, dishes of half-eaten food littered the concrete next to a Dumpster. A dozen cats swarmed around the food. A short man in a dirty white T-shirt, his belly protruding under a filthy apron, stepped out of a door and lit a cigarette. The cats ignored him. He stacked a couple of the empty dishes to take inside, straightened and noticed Gil.

"*Qu'est-ce que tu fais ici?*" he demanded.

Gil froze. Damn. He should have stayed hidden.

"I don't speak—"

"American," the man said in English. He spat. "What are you doing here?"

Gil hesitated. He needed to be faster on the uptake. But the man's eyes softened.

"Lost, eh?"

That was almost too easy. Gil nodded. He could make pity work for him.

The man threw the lit cigarette toward the cats. "Come with me." He stepped back into the building.

For a moment, Gil wondered whether he should walk the other way. He glanced up at Mount Royal and the darkened windows of the buildings all around. He didn't have anywhere else to go. The man seemed friendly enough. And maybe Gil would find a restroom. He entered the rear of a diner.

The man had placed the cats' dishes into a suds-filled sink and was rinsing his hands under running water.

"I'm Tony," he said. "What are you called?"

"Gil."

"Take a seat." He waved to the stools by a long counter.

Gil sat on the one closest to the kitchen. The diner was still dark, but a woman stood just inside the kitchen door, her hair under a net, chopping up a huge pile of peeled potatoes. She squinted at Gil as he sat down.

"Another stray?" she asked Tony.

"Just a kid," Tony said. "Here," he added, pushing a cardboard cup filled with coffee toward Gil, "and don't worry about Renée. She likes to be grumpy."

"Thank you," Gil said.

He reached for his pouch, figuring Tony would probably take an American bill. Tony raised his hands.

"On me," he said.

Tony plopped a gallon of milk and a container full of sugar next to the cup. "You'll like it pale and sweet."

How did Tony know?

"Thanks," Gil said again.

Tony returned to the sink. He quickly rinsed a whole load of dishes and placed them into a large plastic rack, any which way they fit.

"We should fire Adèle," he said.

"I did," Renée said.

Tony looked at her for a second, then lifted the filled rack and placed it over several others in an industrial dishwasher. He shut the machine's door, pushed a few buttons, and Gil heard the muffled whoosh of water and steam.

"They'll be dry before lunch," Renée said, "and we have enough for the morning rush."

Gil heard the front door scrape open, then its lock click back into place. A tall, angular, gray-haired woman appeared in an off-white waitress dress with matching shoes.

She dumped her large handbag into a tiny cupboard beneath the soda machine and locked it in with a key she kept around her neck. She granted Gil only one glance before gathering ketchup bottles from tables. She was obviously used to stray teenagers drinking coffee at the counter before the diner opened.

"You fire Adèle yet?" she asked Renée as she unscrewed all the bottles and began refilling them.

"When I came in," Renée said.

Gil drained the last of his coffee. It was time to leave. He stood, hoisting his duffel onto his shoulder. Tony was now at the griddle, where he'd dumped a huge mound of chopped onions.

"Thank you," Gil said. "I should get going."

"At this time of the morning?" Tony said. "Where are you off to in such a hurry?"

Both women stared at Gil. He squared his shoulders.

"To find a bank."

"To rob it?" Renée asked, pointing at the duffel with her knife.

Gil's anger flashed. "Of course not. I need to exchange money."

"Ah," Tony said. He pushed the onions around.

Gil had made it halfway to the back door when Renée, who was now coring green peppers, piped up.

"It'll be three and a half hours before it opens."

"I know that," he said. Truthfully he had hoped it'd be sooner. But still. "I need to find it first."

"Two doors to our left," Renée said.

Gil now felt foolish. What was he going to do for the next several hours?

The waitress, who had begun refilling saltshakers on her tray, must have read his mind. She pointed to a door between the women's and men's restrooms. "You can store the duffel in the closet. Then you can help me with these."

Gil hesitated.

She placed the box of salt on the counter, took another key from her neck and unlocked the door. "No one will bother it."

Gil did owe them a coffee. And if he put some time in

here, maybe he'd score some breakfast, too. He gave the waitress one of his nicer smiles.

She told him to call her Richeline and handed him a spare apron. He spent the next half hour distributing salt-shakers, gathering and filling sugar jars and placing packets of jam, honey and syrup into baskets Richeline placed in front of him. By six, bleary men and women began trickling in. Most asked for a coffee to go, with a danish or bagel, but some were taking seats at booths and at the counter. Renée had changed into a new apron and joined Richeline in the bustling dining room, taking orders, serving breakfasts, managing the register, as Tony cooked up one order after another at lightning speed. Gil rinsed dirty dishes in the deep sink and filled racks, ready to load into the dishwasher when the clean dishes cooled down enough to be removed. He fetched anything Tony asked him to, and when the rush subsided sometime around nine-thirty, Tony placed a plate heaping with scrambled eggs, home fries, two pancakes, four pieces of bacon and two slices of buttered toast onto the counter.

"Give the apron to Richeline," he said.

Gratefully, Gil handed her the now-damp cloth.

She smiled. "Eat up. You earned it."

Renée nodded as she cashed out a customer farther down the counter.

In the craziness of his impromptu role as dishwasher and gofer, Gil had forgotten how hungry he was. He gobbled down the breakfast, appreciating why the diner had such a large flow of customers in the morning. He scraped the last of the eggs with the remains of his toast and rose to bring the plate back into the kitchen.

"I'll do that," Richeline said. She handed him the duffel bag.

"The bank should be open now," Renée said.

Gil paused. He might need to spend a couple of days in the city. Extra cash would help him get by.

"I was wondering," he said, "if you need an extra set of hands. . . ."

"Nope," Tony said from the griddle. "Can't hire you. Illegal, you know. But if you need breakfast, you come here. We'll fix you up."

Gil exited through the front door, surprised by the street bustle after the quiet earlier that morning. He looked up. An old sign outlined in pink neon announced, "Apropoulis"—his passage, he realized, into the city.

9
Into the cave

Gil stepped forward and collided with a skinny woman in a pink shirt coming his way.

"Fais 'tention!" she said.

Gil didn't know what that meant, but by the tone and her scowl, she hadn't appreciated the bump.

"Sorry," he said.

She picked up the purse she had dropped, gave him another scowl and strode into the Apropoulis. Gil shook his head. It was as much her fault as his. He rehoisted his duffel and headed for the bank.

He joined a short line. When Gil got to the teller, she smiled politely.

"Je peux vous aider?"

"Do you speak English? I'm American."

"Of course," she said with a heavy Québécois accent. "How can I help you?"

Gil took out his pouch and placed two hundred and fifty dollars on the counter. "Can you convert this for me?"

She nodded. "Do you have the identification?"

He decided to use his driver's license rather than his passport, since the photo was more recent. She looked at it and read the birth date.

"A student exchange?" she asked.

"Yes," he lied.

"One minute," she said.

As she went back with the cash, counted it out and filled in some forms, Gil glanced to his right. A woman was handing over a piece of paper—a check, it looked like—to the teller next to him. She wore jeans, flip-flops and the pink button-down shirt that had caught his eye earlier. She was the woman he had bumped into.

"You sign here," his teller said.

She counted the Canadian cash, a rainbow of bills and several coins. He carefully folded the bills into his pouch and pocketed the coins. He reached down for his duffel and noticed that the woman in the pink shirt was now by the bank's front door. She had narrow features, dirty blond hair tied back into a ponytail and small, round eyes that were staring at him. As he approached her, she smiled, which made her look quite beautiful.

"I waited," she said in accented English, "because I want to say sorry."

He held the door for her. "It's okay. We both bumped into each other."

"*Oui,* but I was . . . how do you say? Brusque?"

Gil smiled. Yes, she had been brusque.

"I make it up, okay?" she said.

"Sure." Gil grinned, glad his charm still worked here in Quebec.

"I treat you to a *café, non?*"

"Thanks."

She led him farther down the street and turned up a block where a small coffee shop, with two tables out front, advertised espresso in its window.

"How you like it?" she asked.

"Milk and sugar," he said.

She ordered for them at the counter and brought the steaming cardboard cups to one of the small tables. She took a sip from hers before extending a hand.

"We need the introductions," she said. "I am Adèle."

The name sounded familiar.

"Gil Marsh."

Her hand was soft in his.

"You are American, *non?*"

"Yeah."

"Un étudiant?"

Gil had taken a year of French in eighth grade, but he had forgotten most of it. And when she said *"ay-tu-DZEE-aw,"* he had no idea what she meant. "I'm sorry, I don't know any French."

"Oh. That is okay," she said. "I only ask if you are a student."

This was a natural question, he realized. "Yeah. But I don't start till after Labor Day." That gave him almost two weeks. He had been working on this story line since the teller had asked him.

"Aah. So you are a free man." She said this with a wave, as if to encompass the whole world.

Gil laughed. "As free as a poor man can be."

"*Eh oui. Un étudiant,* he not have a lot of money."

Gil shrugged, but she was right. He had a fair amount of cash at the moment, but he needed to make it last.

"Where are you staying?" she asked.

Gil thought quickly. "At a youth hostel—until my dorm room opens up."

"I have an idea," she said. She smiled, crinkling the small ridges around her blue eyes. They were so pretty! "I just lose my roommate. I need someone permanent, but until the school begin, you can rent the room. If you want."

Gil wasn't sure about that. Rooms were expensive: he had seen the ads in the Green Valley paper—many hundreds of dollars a month. He couldn't afford that.

"No worry," she added. "You come take a look first, then you decide."

Gil was less and less certain, but Adèle seemed determined.

She rose, coffee cup in hand. "You okay for a walk?"

He laughed. A walk was nothing. And he did need a bed for tonight. "Lead the way."

She did. A long way. They walked away from the mountain, heading down a wide avenue—Sherbrooke, it was called. They passed tall, shining buildings with banks and fancy shops that slowly shortened to buildings of gray stone and brick, gas stations and apartment buildings. They turned left, up Boulevard Saint-Laurent. The street was grungier. Garbage and urine smells escaped from alleys. Bums who hadn't washed in weeks sat on street corners. A woman with a small kid begged from a doorway. Gil reached into his pocket and pulled out a silver coin with a golden circle embedded in its center. It looked like play money. He put it in her outstretched hand.

"*Merci, monsieur!*" she said with emphasis.

Adèle raised an eyebrow.

When they had gone another block, she said, "You are a generous student."

Gil shrugged. What was the big deal?

"That was a toonie," she added. "Two dollars."

Gil felt like an idiot. He needed to be more careful. "I'm still not used—"

She put a hand on his arm. "That okay. Two dollars, that's not so much. Just remember. The Canadian coins are real money."

They turned right down one street, left on another. Gil became disoriented after the fourth or fifth turn. They wound through blocks of buildings a few stories high that sported long metal stairways to their upper floors. Adèle stopped at a weathered, two-story yellow row house, paint peeling off the stairs, and pulled out a key. She walked down two sunken steps to a weather-beaten door next to a trash can.

"*Voilà,*" she said, leading him into a dimly lit apartment.

She turned on a light in the tiny living room, which connected to an even smaller galley-style kitchen. She threw her purse onto the table that filled one side of the room.

"Your room is this way," she said.

She led him to a door in the back, pointing out a dingy bathroom on the way.

"It is small," she warned.

That was an understatement. The room was no larger than a utility closet. A bare mattress took up most of the floor. A green paper lantern covered the ceiling bulb, giving the yellow walls a sickly tinge. There was just enough room for two people to stand, if they didn't mind rubbing elbows.

Adèle gave him a wry smile. "You see why my roommate left."

Gil grinned.

"I know you don't have much money," Adèle continued, "but if you give me fifteen dollars a week, it would help me pay for the electricity and telephone."

That, Gil thought, was a fair price. It was less than it would cost him for one night in a hostel! He dropped his duffel in the back corner and extended his hand. "Deal."

She gave him another of her dazzling smiles and shook his hand. He pulled out his money pouch, carefully counted out one blue five-dollar bill and a purple ten and handed them to Adèle. She tucked the bills into her wallet.

"Now," she said, "I need to find a job. So you need to keep busy without me."

"A job?"

"Fired," she said matter-of-factly. "Early this morning. I don't fill the saltshakers the way they like."

A bell went off in Gil's head. Of course, the Adèle that Renée had fired from the Apropoulis. He watched her as she laid out a newspaper on the table and began circling ads with a pen.

She paused and smiled up at him. "You are my roommate now. I have an extra towel in the box."

The box was a small plastic crate wedged between the sink and the wall. Gil took the scratchy but clean yellow towel and went back to his room to get clean underwear from his duffel. He'd be able to rinse out yesterday's clothes now.

Maybe Adèle wasn't a great waitress. But she had given him a room. And even if the room was a cave, it was what he needed: a safe place he could afford while he tracked down Enko's grave and figured out how to head north.

After he showered and hung his washed clothes over the shower rod to dry, Gil stretched out on the mattress, just to test it. He immediately fell asleep. He woke up, confused for a moment. His door opened a sliver.

Adèle poked her head in. "You okay? You've been sleeping a long time."

Gil stretched. "Yeah. I feel great."

But it had been a while since his massive breakfast at the Apropoulis, and his stomach rumbled angrily.

"We go out," Adèle said.

Out? He still hadn't started looking for the cemetery. His stomach growled again.

"I need to get some supper," Adèle added.

That convinced him. He looked down at his rumpled clothes and ran his fingers through his hair.

"You look fine," Adèle said. "Get some shoes." She sounded like his mother.

Gil checked the phone. Four-forty-five. He had slept the afternoon away! He hesitated, remembering the message from his mom. Should he reply? He heard Adèle rummage at the other end of the apartment. She was waiting for him. He tied his sneakers.

Adèle led them to a park surrounded by colorful three-story buildings and filled with young people (real students, he figured), several loose dogs and the smell of reefer wafting from a corner.

"This is Square Saint-Louis," she said.

A couple of guys and a woman, all dressed as latter-day hippies, waved.

"Adèle!" the woman yelled. *"Tu reviens?"*

"Plus tard," Adèle said.

Gil wondered what they had said. Enko had once told him that Montreal was a bilingual city—people spoke both English and French. A tourist from the United States could easily get around. But he realized that he wasn't a tourist. He wasn't sure exactly what he was—a stranger in a new land. He had fled Green Valley, looking for answers. He'd need to learn some French—he could use a dictionary.

"What did she say?" he asked.

Adèle looked at him for a minute. "She asked me if I come back."

"And you said?"

Adèle smiled. "'Later.'"

Gil nodded. He wouldn't mind returning to the park.

They reached a street that had been closed off to traffic. Tables lined the sidewalks, spilling out from dozens of restaurants. Gil's mouth watered at all the food smells.

"You ever have *poutine*?" Adèle asked.

"Poo-teen?"

"No translation for that," Adèle said. "You are going to get a treat."

She led him past the sit-down places, around the corner to another street where a hole-in-the-wall restaurant advertised *"Frites"* in its window. At the counter, Adèle ordered a hamburger "all dressed" and a *poutine*. The woman rang up the order. *"Douze et cinquante,"* she said.

Adèle reached in her purse and her face fell. "I remember my coins, but left my wallet at home." She showed Gil the change purse and took out a toonie and two quarters. "You have ten dollars we could use?"

"Sure."

He handed her a twenty-dollar bill, which she passed on with the coins to the server. Adèle gave the ten dollars change to Gil.

"I pay you back when we get home," she said.

"No problem," Gil said.

They sat at a small booth, and soon the server called them from the counter. Adèle returned with a tray. She placed the *poutine* in front of Gil with a plastic fork and paper napkins while she unwrapped the hamburger for herself. The *poutine* looked like an unholy mess: french fries with what Gil thought might be melted cheese, covered in a brown gravy.

"They make the best *poutine* this side of Saint-Laurent," she said. "Try it."

To Gil's surprise, it tasted good. The fries were delicious, moister and less grainy than the ones he got at diners in the United States. The cheese was very fresh and creamy. The gravy tasted rich and pulled it all together. And the dish was filling! He finished everything in the Styrofoam bowl.

Adèle smiled at him. "Good stuff, *oui?*"

"*Oui,*" Gil said.

"So. You're no student."

Gil was taken aback by the matter-of-fact way she said it. "How did you know?"

"Easy. No books. No laptop. No papers. No pens. An American like you, he comes with TV, stereo, car, twenty suitcases *and* a laptop. Always the laptop."

Gil frowned.

"That okay," Adèle continued. She took another bite from her hamburger.

"It's a long story," Gil said.

"I'm not in any hurry."

"A *really* long story."

Adèle put her hamburger down. "Okay. I finish the hamburger. We get two Pepsis and we go back to the Square. I find a quiet corner, and you tell me the story. Maybe I can help."

Gil didn't reply. Adèle didn't seem to expect him to. She methodically finished her burger, dabbed her lips with her napkin, gathered all the dishes and dumped them in the corner trash. She bummed a few more dollars from Gil for sodas, and they headed back the way they had come, winding their way to the park. The whole while, Gil kept running through his head the last thing she had said. "Maybe I can help."

Gil started slowly, describing his first meeting with Enko. Adèle listened intently. Her face didn't even twitch. She nodded sometimes and let Gil speak. And as he warmed to the story, he forgot she was there, sitting in the shadows of tall trees on a bench, smoking a cigarette, surrounded by homeless vagrants, partying students and lovers.

He told her how he loved Enko, and how Enko had died. He described his grief and how he couldn't stay in Green Valley anymore. The sun had set by the time he finished the tale.

Adèle pressed a hand over his and gave it a squeeze before taking it back. "I am sorry."

Gil stared at his hand. He could still feel the press of her fingers. The ring glinted slightly in the light of the streetlamps. Gil told her about the legend.

"That is quite a story," Adèle said.

"Yeah. But it made me think that I should head north."

Adèle laughed. "North is big."

Gil looked down at his hand. "First I'll find Enko's grave."

"And after that?"

Gil thought for a moment. He wasn't ready to tell her

about searching for the immortal man. She'd laugh at that, he was sure. "I'll go to where they made this ring. The ring connects me to Enko's family."

"Can I see it?" she asked.

Gil hesitated but slipped the ring off his finger. She took it, stubbed out her cigarette and stood, taking a few steps toward the streetlamp. She lifted the ring to get a better view and twisted it. Gil saw the light reflect off the stone. When Adèle returned, she handed the ring back to him.

"A dark stone," she said.

"Do you know anything about it?"

"No."

"Do you know someone who might?"

Her hesitation made Gil hopeful.

"Let me think on it."

10
Maurice

The next morning, Gil woke to shouting. He heard Adèle's voice in a high-pitched, rapid-fire French, answered by a rumbling, deep voice, not quite as loud, but menacing in its tone.

Gil bolted out of bed, pulled on his jeans and tiptoed out of his bedroom. As he approached the front of the apartment, he saw Adèle from behind, her legs planted apart, head held high, a finger pointed at a large man whom Gil saw from a three-quarters angle. The man wore torn jeans and a stained short-sleeve shirt that hung, untucked, over his stomach. A patch of stubble dotted one cheek, while his unruly hair stood up in all directions. The palm of his left hand lay flat on the kitchen table, as though he had just made a forceful point.

"What's going on?" Gil said.

Adèle whirled. Her face boiled in fury. Her eyes, her nose, her mouth, her cheeks, all were pinched and angry. "Gil."

69

The man looked over at Gil in mild surprise. *"Un autre?"*

"What's going on?" Gil repeated.

Adèle took a deep breath, and Gil watched as she forced her features into neutrality.

"I am sorry. Some people have no manners," she said.

"C'est qui, ça?" the man asked. He appeared more curious than angry.

Adèle swung back around. "Gil, this is Maurice." She paused. "My old roommate."

The man now grinned. It wasn't a friendly grin, but it wasn't malicious, either.

"Hello, Maurice," Gil said.

The grin grew. "An *anglo?*" He stared at Gil, assessing the bare chest and hastily put-on jeans. "At least you're a pretty one."

Gil frowned and clenched his fists. "I'm here temporarily."

"Of that, I'm sure," Maurice said.

His Québécois accent sounded thicker than Adèle's but his speech was more fluid. He seemed genuinely amused by the situation.

Adèle frowned. "Maurice is leaving."

Gil took another step forward, placing himself next to Adèle. If she needed his help, he was there. But Maurice focused on Adèle and made no move to leave.

"Your new boyfriend doesn't change anything."

Adèle jutted her chin out as if she didn't care. Maurice pursed his lips, then turned to go. At the front door he paused, glanced back at Gil and left. The door clicked behind him. Adèle exhaled and crumpled onto a chair.

"Thank you," she said.

Gil sat across from her. "What was that all about?"

Adèle sighed. "When Maurice left, we had a fight. He thinks it is not over, the fight."

The man was at least twice her size.

"Do you need me to—"

"*Non, non,*" she interrupted. "Maurice will not hurt me. He just doesn't like to give up the argument. He'll get over it." She placed a hand on one of Gil's. "We know each other since we were little kids at Marieville. He is like a little brother who always gets in the way."

Gil gave her a wry smile. "He had a crush on you?"

Adèle smiled back, making those blue eyes of hers crinkle. "Yes. A crush. Some things, they don't change."

Gil still didn't know what they had argued about, but Adèle's obvious ease with the subject convinced him it couldn't be that serious.

"I am just sorry," she said, "that you have to meet this way."

"Oh?"

"I was hoping to ask Maurice for help."

Now Gil was curious. "Help?"

But instead of answering, Adèle rose, headed over to the galley kitchen and began emptying a small grocery bag. Gil had briefly thought about getting breakfast at the Apropoulis, but Adèle placed a liter of orange juice and a loaf of sliced bread on the table. She also took out her wallet and handed Gil a five-dollar bill, a toonie and a one-dollar coin called a loonie. "For the hamburger and Pepsi," she said.

She poured Gil a small glass of juice and put a plate in front of him while she boiled water for instant coffee.

"Maurice knows a lot about jewelry," she said.

Gil had trouble believing it—this oversized man in cheap, beat-up clothes?

"You not believe, I can tell. But it's true. Right now he is a student at the *Université de Montréal*, in their engineering. But always, when we were growing up, he love the rocks. He study them and collect them."

A geology geek. That would make sense.

"I think he might tell us something about your ring."

That seemed somewhat of a leap to Gil.

"But right now," she continued, "he be too angry with me to help. So first, we look for your friend's grave."

We? Gil was surprised but pleased, too. He crammed down a half dozen slices of bread while she fetched a laptop from her bedroom and turned it on.

"So," she asked, "where is he buried?"

"Uh, here, in Montreal."

"*Oui.* But where in *Montréal*?" She pronounced it *moh-ray-al*. "It's a big city."

How could Gil be so stupid? Green Valley had only one cemetery, not too far from the high school, near the town green. It was big and old and had lots of trees. Kids dared each other to go there at Halloween. Gil never thought much about it. But here in Montreal, there were probably dozens!

"I don't know which one," Gil said.

Adèle stared at him for a moment, unbelieving.

"This will be a little more work," she said.

She asked Gil to spell Enko's name for her, then typed it into the search engine. "Maybe we are lucky and there was an announcement that would tell us where he was buried. Or give us the name of a church or the . . . uh . . . place where they take care of the details. You know."

"The funeral home?"

"*Oui.* That's it."

Several articles from the Green Valley paper came up: three in its sports section about the high school cross-country team, plus one about the memorial service back in May. The search also pulled up Enko's defunct Chatbook page. Nothing useful.

"Okay," Adèle said. "We try again."

She typed in *"cimetières Montréal."* That pulled up a long list next to a map with arrows indicating each one.

"So," she said, "was he Catholic? Protestant? Jewish? We can narrow it down that way."

Of course—cemeteries were usually divided by religion. Why hadn't Gil thought of that? But they had never talked about religion—not that Gil remembered.

He tried to visualize Enko's house. When he visited, they spent most of their time in Enko's room. He had a vivid memory of Enko's computer, his game system and his bed. Gil shut that memory down, concentrating on the Labettes' kitchen and living room. The house was much like everyone else's, but he did recall seeing an old cabinet with photos inside— one being a picture of a baby after a baptism.

"He was baptized."

"Catholic? Anglican? Pentecostal?"

"I don't know."

Adèle was undeterred. "Okay. His family, they were just *Québécois* or did they also have English roots?"

"Québécois, I think."

"Well, that is a start."

Adèle concentrated on the Catholic cemeteries first—because most Québécois were from Catholic backgrounds. She took out her cell phone and offered to make the calls. "Since you don't speak French."

"Thanks!" Gil meant it.

Two cemeteries had interred people with the name Labette, but neither had any record of Enko. Adèle started down the list of other Christian cemeteries, then contacted non-denominational ones. As the morning gave way to the early afternoon, she called back the ones where no one had been there the first time. Still no luck.

Soon, the only burial grounds left were Jewish and Islamic ones.

"Are you sure he was buried in *Montréal?*" Adèle asked, sounding defeated.

She had made so many phone calls and looked tired. Gil was grateful for her patience. She had not complained once about this monumental chore, rather reassuring him each time that the next call might produce the information they needed.

"That's what I thought," he said.

He had been told that the family plot was in the Montreal area. But that could be anywhere, he realized. The area was huge. How was he going to track Enko down? He was too late now to contact Enko's parents for more specifics—they would alert his parents, who must still think him safely with the cross-country team.

He buried his face in his hands.

Adèle leaned over and put a hand on his arm. "*Voyons*. We'll figure something out." She glanced up at the clock. "It's getting late. I promised some friends to meet them at a pub on Saint-Denis."

She invited him along. Gil realized he had never told her his age—she had never asked. And in Quebec, the drinking age was eighteen. At home, Robert usually supplied the booze with the help of his older brother. Here, he should be able to pass.

The pub was a long underground room with tables along one wall and a bar along the other. To Gil's relief, they also served food—sandwiches, fries, nachos. Several tables had been pushed together, and a group of a half dozen men and women greeted Adèle as she walked in. Maurice sat among them. He gave Adèle and Gil a nod.

Everyone spoke French. Adèle introduced Gil, but after the initial "Hello" and "You are from the U.S.?" they lapsed back into French. He gave his order to a waitress, glad to have food and beer to keep busy. When he had almost finished eating, Maurice moved over and sat next to him.

"How did you meet Adèle?" he asked.

Adèle glanced up from her conversation on the other side

of Gil, but the woman she was speaking to leaned in and said something in her ear that distracted her.

"At a bank," Gil said, "after I knocked her over on the sidewalk."

"Ah," Maurice said.

"We struck up a conversation, and I told her I needed a place to stay."

"So she showed you her extra room."

Gil grinned. "Yeah."

Maurice lowered his voice, leaning in. "I've known Adèle a long time. Be careful."

Gil sat back. Adèle, so far, had been nothing but helpful to him. She had spent all morning tracking down Enko—even if they hadn't been successful.

"She's okay." He said it a little louder than he had intended.

Adèle looked over with an inquisitive smile. "Maurice tell you stories about me?"

Maurice laughed. "Not yet!"

A man with a black goatee leaned across the table. "You tell us."

"No, no," Maurice said. "Only Adèle gets to tell you about Adèle."

Adèle sat up straight in mock seriousness. "*Absolument!*"

Laughter all around.

Then the woman next to her said something in French to the young man, and pretty soon they were all talking and laughing again—in French. Maurice, however, didn't join them. He was watching Gil.

"You have an unusual ring," he said.

Gil flattened his hand. "It was given to me."

"Would you mind if I looked at it?"

Gil remembered what Adèle had told him earlier. "Sure."

Maurice's touch was surprisingly gentle, despite his thick fingers. He fished an eyepiece from a shirt pocket and wedged it into his right eye, bringing the stone under a lamp that hung next to him. He turned the ring slightly right and left, grunting as he did. Then he flipped the ring around and inspected the setting. Adèle winked at Gil and went deeper into conversation with her neighbor.

Maurice popped the eyeglass out, stowed it in his pocket and held the ring out for Gil to take back. He gave Gil a look of genuine curiosity.

"Do you know anything about it?" he asked.

"My friend gave it to me before he died," Gil said. "The ring belonged to his family. There's a legend that goes with it."

Maurice leaned forward. "Can you recount it for me?"

So Gil did. He told the story of doomed love and of a ring made by an immortal man.

"'Antoine et Clotilde,'" Maurice said. "Yes, I have heard that tale, too. Were you ever told how Antoine died?"

"Only that he was inconsolable and died the following spring."

Maurice sat back. "There's more to it than that."

Now Gil leaned forward.

During Clotilde's wake, Antoine refused to leave her coffin's side. His father had to drag him home from the cemetery after the burial. Antoine took to carrying the ring around with him wherever he went. When men headed north to the lumber camps, Antoine signed up.

"You're not strong enough," his father said. "You've never done this kind of work."

"I'll find my place," Antoine said.

The jobber quickly assessed his worth. He paired him with a seasoned lumberjack who had brought two draft horses with him. Antoine proved good with the horses, so as soon as the cold truly set in, the crew boss put them to icing.

"What's icing?" Gil asked.

Maurice explained that to transport logs to launching points by riverbanks and lakeshores, the workers dragged them on heavy sleighs. Overnight the icing crew drove a double sleigh loaded with a large tank filled with water, which they spread over the trails, allowing ice to form. Once the barrel was empty, they'd refill it at a lake and repeat the process until dawn. They iced the trails as thoroughly as they could for the crews to slide along come morning.

"It sounds like exhausting work," Gil said.

Maurice nodded.

The work suited Antoine.

Although perpetually tired and cold, he only had to deal with the older lumberjack. He, in turn, proved taciturn. They slept during the day and hardly spoke at night. Antoine brooded about Clotilde in silence.

Come spring, his normally quiet partner began talking about home. He hoped to be back in time for lambing and wondered whether his youngest had begun walking. Antoine's heart hardened at this talk of home life. He had lost the only woman he would ever love. He'd never have a home to call his own.

When the jobber started asking for *draveurs,* Antoine signed up. His partner tried to talk him out of it.

"A *draveur?*" Gil asked.

Maurice explained. In spring, they released the walls of logs that the lumberjacks had piled up. These tumbled into the water to begin a long route down swollen streams and lakes, to reach mills or to be exported to England. On lakes and larger rivers, the flotillas of logs were corralled into log booms—sixty-foot-long floating chains of logs linked to each other. The *draveurs* manned the big boats that pulled the logs along. On smaller rivers, the logs were set loose. Sometimes they floated easily, and sometimes they cascaded down, roaring and thwacking in a deafening cacophony of wood slamming on wood. The *draveurs'* job was to keep the flow going, pushing and pulling with long poles and peaveys—javelins with a hinged hook.

"It sounds dangerous," Gil said.

Maurice nodded again.

Inevitably, the logs jammed. These were the most dangerous times. Logs had to be pulled free. Sometimes explosives were used to blow the jam away. Antoine always ran into the thick of the work.

At a particularly treacherous set of rapids, the swollen river had almost overtaken the banks. The current frothed, running swift, freezing and deadly. At the top of the rapids, a jam formed. Though it was still small, if they didn't loosen it immediately, the logs would back up for several miles.

Antoine ran to the pile. No one could stop him. He pushed and pulled as more experienced men yelled at him to stop and wait for help. They wanted to string a rope, use longer poles. This was no place for a man by himself.

The men who watched that day said they saw glee in Antoine's eyes as he pried the logs loose. At the pop of the freed logs, Antoine raised his arms in victory and, for the first time since he came to the lumber camps, he smiled. And then he went under.

They found his body downstream, barely recognizable, crushed and battered by the logs.

Gil shuddered at this story.

"What happened to the ring?"

"The legend says that the undertaker found it, sewn into

the hem of Antoine's shirt. It was a miracle that it hadn't been lost when he was killed."

"That seems incredible."

Maurice grinned. "It's all a legend. Now see here." He pointed to the stone in Gil's ring. "This is *grenat*—garnet, from northern *Québec*. Good quality. The setting is old and a bit rough, done by someone with rudimentary tools but with true craft. I would guess the *forgeron* made jewelry on the side."

"For-juh-ROH?" Gil asked.

"A blacksmith. Every village needed one. But the metal is impure—you can see the streaks."

"Would you know where it was done?"

Maurice frowned. "No. But if I were looking, I'd start in the *Laurentides,* at one of the smaller settlements that were around at least one hundred years ago. They used to mine garnet up there by Le Gros-Curé."

"Luh-groh-coo-RAY?"

"It's a village, about a hundred and sixy kilometers north-west of *Montréal.*"

Gil thought about that for a moment. "Do you think it was really made by an immortal man?"

Maurice burst out laughing. Adèle looked over, curious. Gil frowned, annoyed.

"Gil, it is a *legend*. True, that ring is old. And the story is a good one. But . . ." He paused. Gil waited. Maurice shook his head. "Every garnet ring in *Québec* comes with that story."

11

North

Gil walked silently through the evening gloom on their meander back to Adèle's apartment.

"Maurice, he tell you quite a bit. *Non?*"

Gil yanked himself out of his thoughts. "Yes."

"What did he say?"

"He filled me in on the legend."

"He knew about it?" She sounded excited.

Gil recounted what Maurice had told him.

"But then," she said, "this must be the same ring!"

"Maurice said everyone who has a garnet ring is told this story."

"But not everyone has a ring made by a blacksmith, all the way in the *Laurentides,* over a hundred years ago. Even Maurice said the silver was old and the garnet was probably from that area."

Yes, Gil thought. It did all fit.

"What you need to do," Adèle said, "is find the old smith shop."

"But Maurice said it was only a legend."

Adèle shrugged this aside. "Of course he say that. He don't like to believe in those things that aren't *scientifique*."

They passed a convenience store with the word *"Dépanneur"* on a sign above.

Adèle turned in. "I finish my last cigarette," she explained.

She asked for a pack from the man behind the counter. When he rang up the sale, she pulled out her wallet and her face fell. *"Ah non!"*

Gil saw that she no longer had any cash.

"I can take care of it," he said.

"But you don't even smoke. . . ."

"No. It's okay. You've helped me so much."

She took the ten-dollar bill, paid for the cigarettes and handed him the change.

"Thank you," she said, lighting up outside. "It's a very bad habit, I know, but I can't give it up."

The laptop was still on the table when they returned to the apartment, reminding Gil of their defeat.

Adèle unplugged it and stored it in her room. "Maybe tomorrow we have more luck."

Gil nodded but he had begun to worry. This was his third day on the road. Tomorrow was Friday, and the trip to the Berkshires would be over. His parents expected him home tomorrow afternoon.

Gil had texted his mother back. *Got a ride Fri. Have my key.* But he knew Mom. She'd be home waiting. And when he didn't show up, she'd figure out pretty quickly that he never made the trip. The first place his parents would think of was Enko's grave—they would have to. And they wouldn't have any reason *not* to contact Enko's parents to find out where it was. He might be able to beat them to it, but only if he tracked down the cemetery tomorrow morning.

But even then, that might be too late. Wherever Enko was buried, it probably wasn't on the island of Montreal. Gil had to figure out transportation to the cemetery, and that took time. True, there was no way his parents could travel north fast enough to get there before him. But what if his dad called the police and had someone waiting for him? Once they found him, they'd drag him home.

He sat on his mattress, staring at the stark walls. There was no way he was going home. He couldn't bear it. He needed to head north. And maybe Maurice was wrong, and he'd find an immortal man somewhere up there.

Gil turned off the light and stretched out.

He tried to imagine what it must be like to be immortal, to live through every age and see the world change, knowing that as others died, you'd cheated death.

Gil sat up.

How had the man cheated death? He must know something that others didn't, maybe something he could teach Gil. And Gil would use that knowledge to bring Enko back. Then he thought of *Frankenstein* and those cheesy vampire and zombie movies. Could he really bring Enko back, hale and whole? All the stories he'd ever heard told him no. But the immortal man . . . He must know something.

His thoughts were going in circles. What did he want? Gil wasn't sure, but returning home was what he *didn't* want. He needed to leave Montreal, well before his parents got here. He might have already stayed in the city too long.

He closed his eyes. He had to head north tomorrow. Whether or not there was an immortal man, it was where he needed to go.

The next morning, Adèle pulled out her laptop and located Le Gros-Curé for him.

"The best way will be the bus," she said. "You can get a pass—Québecpass, it's called. It's like the European rail pass. You pay almost two hundred dollars, but you can use it as much as you want for four months."

She unplugged the computer. "I go by the station this morning—I have an interview a block away. I can help you get it, if you want."

Gil thought about it. That would leave him about twenty-five dollars—enough to stay in a youth hostel for one night or at a campground for a few nights. He'd find a cash job somewhere and make ends meet. With the pass, he'd be able to travel Quebec for the next four months and sleep on the bus if he needed to. A place to sleep, plus travel. That worked.

"Is there a youth hostel in Le Gros-Curé?" he asked. He remembered seeing several dozen listed for the province when he had looked them up at the library. But he had focused on the ones in Montreal and couldn't remember the names of the other towns.

"It's a big-enough village. There should be one."

Her smile lit up her face. She really was beautiful, Gil thought.

"Okay."

He packed his few belongings. Despite Adèle's generosity, he felt as if he had been cooped up in a cave. Leaving her apartment came as something of a relief. The sun shone, and they decided to walk. Adèle took him past tree-lined, crowded streets and commercial avenues, and at one point made him turn around.

"*Le stade,*" she said.

She pointed to a building in the distance that looked like an enormous horseshoe crab with a large column leaning over its back. He had seen photographs in his parents' tourist guides.

"The Olympic Stadium," he said.

Adèle nodded.

That was a place for athletes. As he had been. As Enko had been, too. He turned his back to the site.

Adèle must have caught his mood because she took his arm in hers. "*Pardon.* I'm sorry. It's just, the building is so famous. . . ."

Gil forced a smile. "It's okay. Let's go."

When they arrived at the bus station, Adèle stopped a few yards from the teller. "Now you can ask him for the Québecpass, but you also ask for the ticket for Le Gros-Curé—they issue a separate voucher after the pass is bought."

Gil nodded.

"In French you say . . ." She enunciated a few sentences. She spoke slowly, but there were too many words, and Gil could make no sense of them. He tried to repeat what she said, but kept tripping up and didn't know what he was saying.

Adèle shook her head. "You not follow."

Gil gave her a sheepish smile.

"That okay," she said. "We do it together. Okay?"

Relief. "Okay."

They approached the teller. Adèle began speaking to the young man in rapid French. She smiled her beautiful smile and the young man smiled back. They talked back and forth, Adèle posing questions, the young man replying and asking several in return.

After a few minutes Adèle turned to Gil. "He wants to know if you go to Le Gros-Curé today because he can issue the ticket with the pass."

Gil nodded. The sooner he left town, the better. Adèle resumed speaking to the teller. The man clicked at his terminal. He said something more, and Gil understood "Gros-Curé."

Adèle turned again. "He asks if you want a one-way passage or round-trip."

"One-way."

Gil might return, but not anytime soon. He knew that. Enko's grave would still be here, and by the time he had found the immortal man, he'd have found a way to track down the grave without tipping off his parents.

Adèle spoke some more. The printer produced paper. The young man said something else.

"With tax, it'll be one hundred ninety-seven and . . ." She turned to the young man and asked something. He replied. Adèle translated, "Fifty-five cents."

Gil took out his wallet. Was he sure he wanted to do this?

The teller spoke to Adèle. She looked at Gil. "He says the next bus will be in forty minutes. The one after is this evening."

That was too late! Gil needed to leave Montreal as soon as possible. He gave Adèle ten twenty-dollar bills. As he stowed the wallet in his pouch, she handed money over and chatted with the teller. A minute later, she stepped aside and walked to a bench. She gave Gil several coins, a ticket for Le Gros-Curé and a long card—the Québecpass. In a corner of the card opposite the provincial flag and French text were the handwritten words *"23 décembre."* A blue seal had been stamped over the date.

"That's the expiration date," Adèle explained. "December twenty-third."

"Thank you," Gil said.

"The man said you need to present the Québecpass at the station to get a ticket to your next destination."

Gil nodded.

They found a fast-food vendor in the station, and Adèle ordered him a *poutine*. She refused to let him pay. "A good trip needs a good meal," she said.

They finished their late breakfast just a few minutes before he was supposed to board.

"Thank you," he told her again. "I don't know what I would have done without you."

She waved and smiled. *"De rien."*

12
Le Gros-Curé

Gil's ride north was uneventful. The bus was only half-full and he had both seats to himself. About a third of the way into the trip, they entered a mountainous landscape—hills really, but with spectacular valleys and tall cliffs. They pulled into towns along the way—Saint-Jérôme, Saint-Sauveur—one saint after another. The houses were unassuming, and the stretches of small businesses, one following the other, reminded him of the Post Road near home.

Sainte-Agathe. Saint-Faustin.

The hills crowded in now. Trees showed some fall colors, while green ski slopes cut ribbons into the hillsides.

Saint-Jovite.

They followed a rust-colored river flanked by farms, which meandered in a valley. Wide sandy beaches filled half the watercourse at the bends. They'd be a nice place to spend a summer day, Gil thought.

La Conception.

Hay bales, gathered into plastic rolls, dotted the fields. The hills were lower now but still rolled on, east and west.

Le Gros-Curé. Finally.

They pulled up at an intersection.

"Is this the bus stop?" Gil asked.

"The only one," the driver said.

Gil thought himself fortunate that the driver spoke English.

Hitching his duffel, Gil disembarked next to a seedy motel. He took a moment to set his bearings. A bronze statue of a very fat priest stood across the street, surrounded by a little park. Just past the motel, the cross street led to a bridge over the river. A few shops and a bank were sandwiched between modest houses in the several blocks on the other side of the highway.

Gil took one look at the motel and decided that he'd prefer inquiring at one of the shops. He crossed over and came to a store with a big sign overhead: *"Quincaillerie."* A variety of knickknacks were in the window, in addition to paint cans, brushes, a few tools and some fishing equipment. He stepped in, and a small-built, middle-aged gentleman greeted him with an offer of help.

"Bonjour! Je peux vous aider?"

"Oui. But . . . uh, do you speak English?" Not for the first time, Gil wished that he spoke more French, or that he had thought to bring a dictionary.

"Of course," the man said. His Québécois accent was very mild.

"I'm looking for the youth hostel," Gil said.

"Youth hostel?"

"Right. You know, where students can stay?"

The man shook his head.

"Rooms are usually very cheap," Gil continued. "And you can get a bunk and a shower."

"No. I'm sorry. Le Gros-Curé doesn't have one."

Adèle had told him the village probably did! "Are you sure? Maybe it's called something else?"

"I've lived here all my life," the man said. "I know what a youth hostel is. We don't have one."

"But Quebec has lots of them!"

The man pulled at an ear. "Well, uh . . . yes. But not in Le Gros-Curé. Maybe in *Montréal*. . . ."

"I just came from Montreal!"

The man pointed to the bridge. "There is camping if you go across the river and down a few kilometers. . . ."

Gil didn't really want to camp. Although the day had been dry, clouds had begun to roll in. He worried that it might rain before morning. He'd prefer a place with some shelter. "Isn't there anywhere I can get a bed for the night?"

The man's face lit up. "The old hotel, across that way, or the motel on the main road."

Gil chose the hotel. The building looked like a big cement block with windows—almost featureless. The word *"Hôtel"* in fading paint indicated its entrance. The lobby was completely nondescript: a counter and a few chairs. A slim woman who reminded him of Adèle sat behind the counter, reading a paperback while snapping chewing gum. She didn't look up until Gil put his arm on the Formica countertop.

"*Oui?*" she said.

"Uh . . . do you speak English?"

Unlike the gentleman from the *quincaillerie,* she seemed offended by the question. She puckered her lips as if the gum had turned sour all of a sudden. "A little."

"I was wondering if you have a room available."

She spent a second appraising Gil, taking in his tousled looks, his bag, his shirt. "Yes."

"How much would it be for one night?"

"Sixty dollars," she said.

Sixty dollars! That was more than he had. "Uh . . . do you have any cheaper ones?"

The woman concentrated on her book. "*Non.* That is the cheapest."

Gil decided to try the motel next to the bus stop.

The man behind the counter spoke English almost as fluently as the first gentleman.

"For how many hours?"

"For the night," Gil said.

How many hours? What kind of a motel was this? The man, with his thin mustache twitching, looked Gil over.

"Seventy dollars," he said.

Gil's stomach sank. "Is there *anywhere* cheaper?"

"You can go camping, across the bridge and down a little way."

Gil found himself back on the main highway. What was he going to do? Maybe Le Gros-Curé was just too small a town. Perhaps in a bigger one, they'd have a hostel.

The man from the *quincaillerie* walked out of his shop

carrying a large box. He accompanied an older woman to a car parked a few yards away. They chatted in French as he stowed the box in the trunk. He waved when she pulled away, then turned and, to Gil's surprise, crossed the street.

"You look lost," he said. "You need a ride to the camping?"

Gil looked down at his shoes. "I was wondering. Is there a bigger town than Le Gros-Curé around here?"

"Of course. If you go south, there is Saint-Jovite—though they call it Mont-Tremblant now."

"How about north?"

The man scratched his chin. "L'Annonciation—about twelve kilometers."

"Does the bus go there?"

"I'm pretty sure. You need a ticket, though."

Gil was thinking fast. If he caught the next bus, he could use his pass, ride up to L'Annonciation and set himself up there. "Do you know when the next bus is?"

"In a few hours. But I don't know the exact timetable."

"Thanks! I'll wait for it."

The man cocked his head. "It will be some time."

"Well, is there somewhere close where I could get something to eat?"

"There's a *casse-croûte* across from the war memorial."

"Thanks."

Gil followed the man's directions, and the little fast-food stand *was* very close—just around the bend on the highway. No one spoke English at the stand. But Gil recognized *"Poutine"* on the board—there seemed to be several varieties. He guessed *"italienne"* must mean "Italian."

"*Poutine* Italian," he told the woman at the counter.

She handed him a Styrofoam dish with french fries, cheese curds and a meat-and-tomato sauce. He grabbed a few napkins and decided to cross over to the war memorial: a large army battery gun next to a parking lot and some picnic tables. He caught a glimpse of the river through bushes, down a little hill. He was grateful for the food—filling, if greasy. He dumped his trash into one of the cans, walked past the public restrooms and decided to follow the boardwalk along the shore. It went out to an overlook over a waterfall. The water level was so low and the boulders so large, he heard more than saw the river between stones. A plaque with old photos of settlers and buildings from the area, titled *"Rivière Rouge,"* gave tourist information, all in French.

A path along the river headed back to the bus stop. Gil followed it. He stopped under the statue of the priest. From this angle, Gil had a clear view of the traffic rumbling down the hill from the south. Some vehicles turned and drove over the bridge. Most curved the other way along the main highway. He planted himself on a bench under the statue, with his bag next to him.

The place felt deserted. One man crossed the bridge. A woman entered one of the houses near the bank. But mostly, Gil watched a steady, though not too heavy, flow of highway traffic. He briefly thought to check his phone for the time, but decided against it. His parents knew by now that he wasn't coming home. They'd be calling him. Best he not even see the messages.

Light had begun to fade when Gil noticed what looked like a bus cresting the tall hill. He rallied and ran to the motel. The bus almost didn't stop—it had passed Gil without slowing down. Luckily the light turned red, and Gil was able to sprint up to the door and knock on it.

The driver seemed surprised.

"Are you taking passengers?" Gil asked.

"*Pardon,*" the driver said. He was a young man—in his early twenties, Gil guessed. "My first week. I lose track of the stops."

"It's okay," Gil said. "I'd like to go to L'Annonciation."

The driver held out a hand. "Ticket, please."

Gil handed him his pass.

"*Qu'est-c'est ça?*" The driver clearly had never seen anything like it.

"A Québecpass," Gil said.

The driver looked at it, turned it over and handed it back to Gil. "Not a ticket."

"But it's good for four months!"

"Sorry. It's not a ticket. You get a ticket, then I can give you a ride."

Of course. Adèle had told him he needed to get the ticket first. Damn.

Gil smiled, turning on the old charm and hoping that the driver would take pity on him. "It's just like one. Couldn't you just give me a ride this time?"

The driver wasn't moved. "Please get off now. You need a ticket for a ride."

An older woman sitting in the front row gave Gil a disapproving, wilting gaze. She clearly thought he was some kind of delinquent.

"Where can I get the ticket?" Gil asked.

The driver pointed behind him. "At the motel."

Gil disembarked and stared at the retreating bus until it disappeared around the bend. Slightly defeated, he entered the motel's rank entrance.

"You want a room now?" the man behind the counter asked.

Gil shook his head. "You sell bus tickets?"

"Yes," the man replied. "But the next one is tomorrow morning. You want to go to *Montréal*?"

"L'Annonciation," Gil said.

"Ah."

The man typed information on a keyboard and a printer clicked and spat out a ticket.

"Eight dollars and seventy-three cents," the man said.

Gil took out his Québecpass and handed it to the man.

"What's this?"

"It's a Québecpass," Gil said.

The man handed it back to Gil. "Eight dollars and seventy-three cents, please."

Gil left the pass on the counter. "This is supposed to cover it. It's good for four months."

The man picked up the pass again and examined it. He flipped it over under the light. "Where you get this?" He sounded suspicious.

"Montreal."

"I mean," the man said, "where in *Montréal*?"

"At the bus station. A friend got it for me."

"Oh." The man placed the pass on the counter again.

"And how much did you pay this friend?" He pronounced "friend" as if it had quotation marks around it.

Gil felt the back of his neck prickle—a hint of worry creeping in. "Just under two hundred dollars."

The man whistled. "That's a lot for a piece of paper from a computer."

Gil frowned.

"Listen," the man said. "There is no such thing as a Québecpass. Your friend played a trick on you."

"But she said that it'd be good for four months. Anywhere in Quebec. Like a Eurail pass."

"We aren't Europe." There was pity in the man's tone.

Gil stared at the pass, not believing what he had been told. "So what do I do with this, then?"

The man lifted his hands, palms up. "Throw it out. Save it for the police. Keep it as a *mémento*. It's not good for much."

Gil grabbed the pass and crumpled it, anger slowly rising as he realized what had happened. Adèle had played him—played him thoroughly. She had stolen most of his cash, two hundred and twenty dollars' worth. In exchange he had gotten two nights' stay in a cave and one *poutine*. Her pretty smiles and generosity had all been a front. What a fool he had been.

He knew where she lived. He could track her down!

But as he thought back, he wasn't sure. Adèle had led him to the apartment each time. And she had always used a different, circuitous route to get there. He didn't remember seeing numbers on any of the doors. And he hadn't paid attention to street signs—he wasn't even sure there had been any around her block.

He could describe her, but she looked like a lot of other Québécois girls he had seen—slim, petite, straight dirty blond hair, blue eyes, a narrow nose. He didn't even know her last name!

"So, you want the ticket?" the man asked.

Gil made a quick calculation. If he bought the ticket, he would have barely enough to scrounge breakfast tomorrow. On the other hand, he wanted to go north, to a bigger town. And L'Annonciation was where he had to go. He took out his wallet and handed over his last ten-dollar bill.

The man counted out the change. "It's coming from *Montréal*. Ten-fifteen. Right in front."

"Thanks."

Gil placed the ticket in his billfold. Where was he going to go now? He exited the motel. Cars and trucks whizzed by. All the shops were closed. Night had fallen, and the air had cooled. Gil dug out a jacket to wear over his sweatshirt and started walking.

He'd have to find a safe place to sleep tonight. He thought about the picnic area off the highway and decided against it. Too many people stopped there. He was likely to be seen. He crossed the bridge over the river and saw a green sign, almost black under the streetlamp: a tent and an arrow. That was the direction to the campground. He followed the arrow.

Houses and side streets petered out. There were no further signs. The road passed through open fields bordered by thick woods and hills in the distance. An old barn stood recessed from the road, near a small farmhouse. The sky above felt enormous in its blackness, stars peeking through the occasional gap in the clouds. The campsite was nowhere to be seen.

Gil had left the last streetlamp more than a mile ago. A pickup, high beams on, passed him, going fast. Gil jumped into the ditch by the road. He realized how lonely and vulnerable he felt. He must have missed a turnoff for the campground at one of those side streets.

The fields around him were rutted and smelled of cow dung. Gil had no hope of finding a dry, sheltered spot here. He decided to retrace his steps, keeping an eye out for signs to the campground. He saw none in this direction either. Perhaps the picnic area was the best choice after all.

As he regained the more trafficked highway, he felt lighter. Yes. He was safer where there was at least some civilization. Fewer cars drove past now, but more trucks, the big eighteen-wheelers and double trailers, most going in the direction of L'Annonciation. It must be a big town.

The parking lot was empty when he got there. A streetlamp illuminated the toilets, and another cast a yellow glow at the other end, by the battery gun. Gil headed for the bushes by the river, hoping for a stone ledge or somewhere else that was dry.

He pushed through a gap to a narrow trail, which he hiked along for a short distance. A sandy patch opened up, four or five feet across, with large bushes curved around it. During the day, it probably offered a nice view of the river. At night, it had just enough shelter on three sides for someone to camp in.

Pleased with his good fortune, Gil pulled out his sleeping bag, plumped up his duffel as if it were a pillow and curled up, his back to the bushes. He'd wash at the water spigot tomorrow, splurge on a box of milk and head to L'Annonciation. He was set!

He didn't hear the feet until they were almost upon him. Two guys had come through the bushes and walked to his sleeping spot. He sat up quickly, and the first man stopped short. He growled something in French.

Gil froze. He could see only their outlines, but these guys were big—tall and wide. The hint of a glint, a reflection of the moon or perhaps a light across the river, came from what looked like a chain on a jacket.

The second guy asked something. The first guy said something back. Gil still didn't know what they were saying, but from their tone, he could tell they weren't happy. Then the second guy pulled out a flashlight, swept the beam across the path and stopped short when he saw Gil. Gil raised a hand to block the beam's glare.

"*Qui es-tu?*" the man demanded.

"Sorry," Gil said, "I—"

"An American!"

How could they tell so quick? They switched to English without a trace of a French accent.

"What are you doing here?" the first guy asked.

Gil shrugged.

The second guy searched the ground with his light, lingering briefly on the duffel before blinding Gil once again.

"You sleeping here?"

The first guy stepped forward, picked up the bag and began emptying it. The phone tumbled out. The man pocketed it.

"Hey! Give that back!"

The man turned on Gil with a smack, sending him sprawling to the ground. "Shut up." He unzipped the toiletry bag and dumped the contents on the ground. "Nothing else."

"The pockets," the man with the flashlight said.

The first man unzipped the duffel's side pockets. He pulled out a snapshot of Gil and Enko, taken at a meet. Gil had forgotten that it was there. The man threw it aside, toward the river.

"That's mine!" Gil yelled.

The man responded with a swift kick to the side of Gil's head. An explosion of pain was quickly snuffed out by total blackness.

When Gil came to, he thought he had gone blind. He could not see anything at all.

Painfully, he dragged his hand up and touched the side of his head. His fingers came away wet. He must be bleeding. He'd need to put something on it. He stretched out his hand, hoping to find his duffel, but instead he scratched himself on the prickly stems of a bush. He had somehow rolled, face-first, up against the bushes.

He heard the roar of motorcycle engines, the screech of tires on the gravel and the sound disappearing into the distance. The men. They had escaped.

He rolled backward and saw stars. His eyes worked fine after all. The moon shone between clouds over the opposite shore, casting a faint light.

Gil was alone. He sat up gingerly. His head hurt at every motion. He scanned the small area, his sleeping nest, and realized that his duffel and sleeping bag were gone. The men must have taken them. He rescued his toothbrush, half out of its case, and a small bottle of acetaminophen that had rolled behind a rock. They had stolen everything else—including his half-used toothpaste and floss and the old toiletry bag.

At least he had been wearing his sweatshirt and jacket. They didn't take those!

That was when he remembered his pouch—the one he kept safely around his neck. He quickly patted his chest, the sudden motion sending shooting pains through his head.

Nothing. Nothing was there. They had stolen that, too!

A feeling of intense violation overwhelmed him: they had pulled him out of his bag, lifted his shirt, patted around his body to find the pouch. They had touched him all over! He wanted to rip his clothes off, jump into the river, wash away his revulsion. But even the thought of moving caused him more pain.

And then it sank in. Nothing was left. No passport. No ID. No money. No change of clothes. Not even the bus ticket to L'Annonciation! He clenched his fist, his thumb reaching up to his ring finger. That was when he noticed that the ring was gone, too.

Enko's ring. His last connection to his friend. Taken by thugs!

Nothing. Nothing. Nothing.

He clutched his toothbrush and bottle of pills and scooted backward while curling inward like an armadillo. He felt the bush's branches poke into him. He pulled the hood of his sweatshirt over his head, shut his eyes and let blackness reclaim him.

13
The crossroad

When Gil awoke, the sun had risen—but Gil wasn't sure where it was. Thick gray clouds blanketed the sky. A misty rain dampened the edge of his hood, the only part of him that wasn't covered by the bush.

Getting out took some effort. The small branches had hooked themselves into the fabric of his jacket, and he had to tug to pry himself loose.

It also hurt. The branches didn't bother him so much, but he had a splitting headache and extracting himself only seemed to make it worse. His limbs felt sore and sluggish, as if his clothes were made of lead. He slowly lifted his hand to the lump on his head where the thug had kicked him. He felt crustiness where his blood must have dried.

He needed to get out of here. The thugs had stolen his phone. They'd see the messages from his parents. They'd figure out pretty quick that he had run away. What if they decided that he was worth something to them? Ransom maybe.

He walked to the gap in the bushes very slowly, even slower than his sluggishness demanded, and stopped.

Although his head hurt and his muscles ached, his hearing seemed particularly acute. He heard the rumble of cars, the downshift of a tractor-trailer, the caw of a crow across the river, answered by another overhead. A child babbled in the distance—in the parking lot—and a woman answered in the twanging tones of Quebec French. He heard their footsteps recede. Doors slammed. A car engine started. Gravel crunched as wheels disappeared onto the highway. Silence. No, not quite. A bird whistled.

Gil stood motionless, listening intently. More cars and trucks rumbled past. Nothing. Nothing else.

As he stepped through the bushes, he heard a loud clap of wood against wood that made him jump. The owner of the *casse-croûte* across the way was opening the building's shutters.

Gil ducked behind the outhouses, not wanting to be seen. The spigot was there, behind a slight rise that encircled the outhouses. He searched his pockets, hoping for a scrap of tissue, anything to wash his face with, but all he found was the useless Québecpass that Adèle had sold him.

If Adèle was her name, he thought.

He stole a roll of toilet paper from one of the stalls. Then, gingerly, bracing for the sting, he dabbed cold water on the side of his head, taking away streaks of brown dirt and dark red dried blood. He used almost the entire roll, until the paper came away clean, then washed his face. He ran his fingers through his hair, hoping that he didn't look too disheveled. He tried to brush the dirt off his jacket and jeans, but under the misty rain, it just smeared. Well, there was nothing to be done.

He drank as much water as he could manage and swallowed two acetaminophen tablets to dampen the headache. Four sleek motorcycles zoomed past, heading north.

Gil crouched behind the outhouses. He remembered the sound of bikes and the glint of a metal chain.

He couldn't stay here. He needed to hike out of town. The man from the store had told him L'Annonciation lay twelve kilometers north. He could walk that. It was a bigger town. Maybe he'd find an odd job there, pay for a bed in a shelter, get something to eat.

The misty rain turned into a light but steady one. Gil pulled his hood back over his head. He had maybe a dollar in coins—the thugs had missed that one pocket—not enough for real food. He pushed the thought away. He wasn't really hungry, he told himself. He had strength enough to follow the highway.

He passed another *casse-croûte,* a couple of gas stations, a cemetery, a few businesses with names that made no sense to him. The road rose and fell. Buildings were few and far apart. A thick, uninviting forest covered any ground not being used for commerce or cultivation. Cars passed him, more trucks, and at one point a bus—his bus, he realized, to L'Annonciation.

He tried hitching, but no one stopped.

He dug his hands deeper into his jacket and plodded on. Then, as he reached blinking yellow lights at an intersection near a small factory, he heard motorcycles again—a deep, loud rumble. He looked up. They were coming from the north. He ducked down into a ditch. They slowed down. Had they seen him? Panic froze him. He watched the two bikers approach.

They rode oversized Harleys, sported black leather with chains across their chests and were tall, burly and bearded. They wore black helmets that looked as though they came from some video game, and had bug-eyed goggles over their eyes. He hadn't seen the men's faces last night, but staring at them now, he was sure: these were the thugs who had beaten and robbed him. They had Enko's ring.

A truck rumbled north, obstructing Gil's view for a few seconds. When it had passed, the bikes had disappeared! He stood tall and now saw them: they had turned right, up the road past the factory, escaping beyond the bend.

Gil only hesitated for a second. Clambering out of the ditch, he crossed the highway and began hiking the cross-road. He was going to get Enko's ring back.

He walked about a mile, winding past wilderness and one lonely house; then the road forked. A sign pointed to the right. "La Minerve." Another pointed to the left. "Lac de Couleurs." Which way did the bikers go?

The road to the right dipped and curved before heading into what appeared to be empty hills, while the one to the left climbed sharply but leveled out. He could see the very top of a roof over the rise. And there were other signs, too—all weathered, one hanging sideways—for businesses whose names he didn't understand. These all pointed to the left.

His hunger had grown, and the headache had returned with a vengeance. The steady rain soaked through the shoulders of his jacket and although it wasn't too cold out, with the rain came chill. Gil needed to find shelter soon. That decided it. He took the left fork.

He plodded on for a while longer, but his legs were so tired. His arms felt like heavy weights. Ahead, recessed a little from the road, a tall maple grew with wide, inviting branches. About half the leaves had turned but almost none had come down yet. He thought there might be a dry patch next to the trunk.

Why Gil stumbled, he didn't know, but his right knee landed hard on rock. Intense pain shot up his leg. The tree was so close. He dragged himself the last few feet and collapsed under the canopy. The ground was dry! Several branches grew out of a knot overhead, and the leaves had funneled the raindrops elsewhere.

The pain in his knee was subsiding. He sat up and leaned back into the trunk, feeling the strength of the ancient maple and the warmth that came with the tree against his back. He let his head sink backward, too, and the wood welcomed him, providing a small cradle for the one spot on his head that didn't hurt. He pulled both knees up. A sharp pinch came from his right knee, reminding him that he had just injured it, but the pain was short-lived. He allowed his arms to fall to his sides. His eyes closed.

The smell. The smell was so comforting. A mix of pine, earth and water. Yes, he smelled the water. Fresh. Not the damp rain, but the lake water that he heard through the drops, lapping up close by.

He woke to a hand gently shaking his shoulder.

"*Voyons*. Wake up. Wake up!"

Gil scrambled backward in fear. He banged his head on the trunk, which sent a new wave of stars through his vision.

The man rocked back on his heels. "It's okay. It's me."

Gil focused.

The short gentleman from the *quincaillerie* crouched across from him. His round face was furrowed in worry, his black hair sprinkled with beads of rain. "You can't stay here, young man."

Gil tried to stand and fell over. His damaged knee seemed to have seized up. His head pounded. And his arms didn't want to do what he asked them to.

The man rushed over and took him by the arm. "Lean on me. My truck is right here."

The man was stronger than Gil expected. Gil stumbled over to the dark blue pickup. It had one of those covers with windows over its bed. The man opened the door and helped Gil hoist himself in.

They drove up and down hills, past occasional houses, following the lake. Gil gripped the door's armrest, trying to focus on the asphalt ahead.

"Someone beat you up?" the man asked.

"Last night," Gil said.

They lapsed into silence, much to Gil's relief. The road

continued for some distance, curving along the water's edge. They drove along the foot of a hill, the ground falling precipitously to the shore on their right, and then climbed past an old, empty gravel lot to a large white-and-blue farmhouse. The man parked the truck around back.

"Come," he said.

With help, Gil stumbled out of the cab. The man led him inside, sat him at his kitchen table and poured him a glass of water, which Gil swallowed in a few gulps. As Gil thanked him, the man placed some cold toast and a tub of grainy white cheese before him, then put the kettle on.

"Eat a little," he said.

It might have been cheap sliced white bread, but the toast tasted delicious. The cheese was a cross between cottage cheese and ricotta—bland but filling.

The man sat across from Gil and put his hands on the table. "Now—"

"Thank you," Gil interrupted.

The man nodded.

"Really," Gil said. "Thank—"

The man raised a hand, interrupting him in turn. "Now we make the introductions."

Gil reddened. He wasn't sure why he was embarrassed, but there was something about the man's gentle formality that made him sit straighter. "I'm Gil Marsh."

"I'm Hervé Durocher. Welcome to my home."

14
The lake

Gil blinked. He looked around. The kitchen opened into a living room. He saw pictures on walls, carpets on the floor, but none of it registered—if asked, he would have been unable to describe what he had seen.

"Thank you," he said again. He couldn't think past his gratitude at being out of the rain and fed.

Hervé Durocher looked him over.

"*Viens,*" he said.

Gil knew that he had just been told to come, and he did try to stand. But his knee wouldn't cooperate. He fell over, catching the table just long enough to slow himself.

Hervé squatted next to him. "Take my arm."

Gil sat up, gathered his good leg under him, took Hervé's arm and, leaning heavily, pulled himself up. Hervé led him to a small room with a metal-framed bed and sat him on it.

"You will need to take off your jeans," he said, "so I can see the knee. Can you manage?"

Gil nodded. Hervé gave him a long look before he stepped out and shut the door.

Gil did not remember what happened next. He must have put his head down to rest for a minute, but when he woke, it was dark out and he was underneath a thick but light comforter that kept him warm. He sat upright, much too fast, and was hit by a wave of dizziness that made him fall back onto his pillow. He shut his eyes, and when he reopened them, light streamed through the window.

This time when he sat up, he felt weak but not dizzy. He swung his legs over and realized that he didn't have any pants on—no shirt, either. Where had they gone?

His momentary panic quickly subsided when he noticed his clothes, clean and folded on a chair near his bed; his dirty sneakers, minus encrusted mud, placed below them; and his jacket hanging off the back of the chair. The bottle of acetaminophen and his toothbrush lay on the side table next to the bed. His right knee was red and slightly swollen. Someone had washed the scrape and placed a small bandage on it. He bent the knee tentatively—it hurt, but he could move it. Slowly he stood. He couldn't put much weight on it, but enough to hobble to the chair and dress.

Someone knocked on the door.

"Gil?" Gil recognized Hervé's voice.

"Come in." He had just finished pulling on his sweatshirt.

"I wasn't sure if you'd need help."

Gil gave Hervé an embarrassed smile. "Were you the one . . . ?"

Hervé raised his hand. "It's okay. You slept through the afternoon and night. My niece, she take care of your knee."

"Niece?" Gil wondered what else had happened that he could not remember.

"No worry. She's a doctor. She looked at your head, too. You may have had a concussion. She said to keep an eye on you."

Bewildered, Gil looked out the window, down to a gleaming lake under rolling hills. A speedboat roared in the distance.

"What day is it?" he asked.

"Sunday," Hervé said.

Gil closed his eyes, confused by the loss of a day, and dizziness grabbed him. He tightened his grip on the chair, and Hervé was next to him, his strong hand holding him up.

"You need some breakfast," he said. "We talk after you eat."

At the mention of food, Gil felt very hungry. Hervé led him back to the kitchen table and served him a small glass of orange juice, half a dozen white-bread toasts, more of the white cheese, some fried eggs and five slices of bacon. Gil ate it all. Hervé gave him a cup of coffee with some sugar and milk, and Gil drank that, too.

Hervé put his own cup down. "So, Gil Marsh. What happened to you?"

Gil stared at this weathered, middle-aged man with his blue eyes and pink cheeks. He had picked Gil up from the gutter, given him shelter, found a doctor for his wounds, washed his clothes and fed him. Gil owed him an explanation.

Without thinking, he felt for Enko's ring and clenched his hand when he realized it was gone. "I'm looking for answers."

Hervé kept his gaze even, waiting for more. Gil looked down at his fist and smoothed it flat with his other hand.

"It's a long story," he said.

Hervé smiled. "It's my day off. I have the time."

So Gil told him—not all, but enough. He told him that his best friend in the world had died and had given him a ring. He told him of his misadventure in Montreal, Adèle's trick, the ticket to L'Annonciation, the mugging, his pursuit of the motorcycle men. Hervé didn't interrupt him, letting Gil pause when he needed it, only sipping coffee and nodding as Gil spoke.

"I was at the end when you found me," Gil said.

Hervé waved that statement away. "You are a healthy young man. Exhausted, yes. Hungry, yes. Bruised and beaten, yes. But you will heal in a few days. *Ce n'est pas sérieux.*"

Gil looked at him inquisitively.

"Nothing serious," he explained.

Gil blushed and looked down at his empty plate. "But all my papers are gone. And the ring—"

"*Oui,*" Hervé said. "Those are concerns. But first you regain your strength. We should contact your parents."

"No!" Gil stood and a pain shot through his knee, forcing him to sit back down. He clutched at the table. "If they find me, I will just run away."

Hervé seemed concerned. "Are they that bad?"

Were they? Gil had to admit to himself that they weren't awful. "They don't understand. And there's something I have to do first."

Hervé tilted his head, inquiring.

"Find where the ring was made."

"And how will you do that?"

Gil sat still, thinking. "I don't know. Not yet. But if they find me, I won't be able to track it down."

Hervé held his gaze for a minute. Gil wasn't sure what he saw, but he gave a slight nod before standing. "Very well. We can start by fixing my *chaloupe*."

"Sha-LOOP?" Gil asked.

"My boat."

As Gil tried to rise again, Hervé put a hand out. "Wait."

He returned with an old wooden cane, solid, with a rubber tip at the bottom. "You use this until your knee heals."

The cane did make it easier to move about. Gil briefly wondered why Hervé had a cane on hand, but he didn't ask. After washing the dishes, Hervé led him out the kitchen door, down a path broken by steps, heading toward the water. The day was beautiful, neither too hot nor too cold. Perfect running weather, Gil thought, if he could run. About ten feet up from the water's edge, a small boat lay upside down on wood blocks.

"My *chaloupe*," Hervé explained. "She has a leak in the front, around one of the rivets, and I need to patch it."

The boat was about twelve feet long, four to five feet wide, made of aluminum. Its sides had been once painted blue but were now weathered, and most of the paint had been scratched away. Deep scratches were etched at the back edge, where a motor must have been attached.

"You sit here," Hervé said, pointing to a stump. He went over to a nearby shed and returned with a large tube. "Soften this." He handed the tube to Gil. For the next fifteen minutes, Gil gently squeezed it until its contents began to soften. Meanwhile, Hervé roughed up the area around the rivet with sandpaper, wiping it clean with a cloth.

"Ready?" Hervé asked.

Gil gave him the tube. Hervé squeezed out a marble-sized amount of dark paste and began kneading it.

"Keep this warm," he said as he handed the tube back to Gil.

Hervé placed the paste over the rivet, spread it quickly and smoothed it over the metal. He covered the sanded area entirely, leaving a uniform layer on the hull. After a few minutes of intense attention, he stepped back. *"Bon."* Then he carefully flipped the *chaloupe* over onto another set of wooden blocks, climbed in and prepped the other side. After receiving another dollop of paste from Gil and smoothing it onto the bottom, he returned the tube to the shed.

"Is that it?" Gil said.

Hervé nodded. "We wait twenty-four hours. It'll set. Then we can put it in the water to test it—but I like to wait an extra day, just in case."

Gil noticed the open drain at the back end. "Won't that let water in?"

Hervé glanced over. "I have a plug. Don't worry."

A pair of Jet Skis zoomed past. Too close, Gil thought. Their wake made the narrow floating pier bob up and down, while waves crashed against the sand and weeds at the shore. Hervé gave them a dirty look but quickly shook it off.

"Come. I show you the family property."

At a pace meant to accommodate Gil's lame knee, Hervé gave him a short tour around the water's edge, then led him to a flowering garden near the house. Although Gil's knee still hurt some, it loosened with the exercise. He could feel the improvement. They sat on a bench overlooking the water. From this vantage point, Gil saw that the lake was much larger than he had realized.

"It's fifteen kilometers long," Hervé said. "That's the south end." He pointed to the left, where hills curved in and water snaked through channels hidden by islands and peninsulas. "Beyond those islands, it's Old Man Miller's land."

No houses were visible there. The shores to the north, on the other hand, were dotted with cottages.

"Who's Old Man Miller?" Gil asked.

"A crotchety old man, not fond of visitors and protective of his land. But the lake is very pretty there. When my *chaloupe* is ready, I'll give you a tour."

That wouldn't be for two days. Gil had to find the bikers and rescue Enko's ring, track down an old smithy and stay ahead of his parents. He had lost an entire day—they were probably in Montreal, looking for him! "I should get going—"

Hervé shook his head. "I am not the doctor, but you bruised that knee bad. It'll take another few days before you'll be able to walk properly."

Hervé was right. But staying? "I've imposed on you. . . ."

Hervé stared at Gil, making him feel uncomfortable. "I took you in. I am responsible."

That surprised Gil.

"It's my duty," Hervé explained. "One man to another."

Gil did not quite understand what he meant, but he was flattered nonetheless. "I'll make it up to you."

Hervé nodded. "*Ben sûr.* But today, we rest. It's Sunday."

Gil willed himself to calm down. Even if his parents had figured out he'd fled to Quebec, they wouldn't be any farther than Montreal. They'd have contacted Enko's parents. Gone to his grave.

He felt a pang. They'd see his grave before he did.

He pushed the thought aside and concentrated on the lake. Boats continued to roar past, going north and south along the main channel. Most were speedboats of various sizes. But he also saw a smattering of pontoon boats, kayaks and a small sailboat. He wondered why Hervé didn't own a nicer boat.

"It's a big property," Gil said. "You're here alone?"

Hervé looked sad all of a sudden. "My wife died of cancer about ten years ago."

That was why Hervé owned a cane, Gil thought. It must have been used by his wife.

"My niece used to stay, but she prefers to live with her fiancé now," Hervé continued.

"I'm sorry," Gil said.

"Thank you. But I'm fine. My son had a few tough years, but he's now at *L'Université Laval* in *Québec* City, so I think he's okay."

He had a son, just a few years older than Gil. Was that why Hervé had been so generous? Did he miss his son, off at school? But this just made Gil worry more about his parents. He pushed this thought aside yet again.

Hervé rose. "Let's get some lunch."

Over ham and cheese sandwiches and sodas on the porch, Gil summoned the courage to ask the question that had been bugging him. "Why don't you have a speedboat?"

Hervé laughed. "You are a young man."

Gil reddened. "But they're faster than your rowboat."

"A *chaloupe* can be fast enough." Hervé eyed Gil with amusement. "Speedboats are expensive and nowhere near as useful. You have to fuss with them every year—polish the chrome, take care of the cushions. . . ." He stood. "Come. Let me show you something."

Gil downed his soda and followed Hervé back through the house and out the kitchen door. Hervé led him up another path, across the road to the barn. He unlocked the padlock and switched on the lights.

A large white *chaloupe* made of wood lay upside down on blocks in the center of the barn. On one side of it were two snowmobiles on trailers, while on the other were some more blocks and an empty space—to store the boat at the water's edge, Gil figured. The rest of the barn was filled with old motors and parts, life preservers, water skis, cross-country skis, snowshoes, sleds and innumerable water toys. Everything had been kept clean—even the gas tanks looked as if they had just been dusted. The paint on the white *chaloupe* gleamed. Gil thought of the battered aluminum of the other boat and couldn't help noticing the contrast.

Hervé laid his hand on the wooden *chaloupe,* gliding his fingers over the hull. "Now this is a real boat. It was built by my grandfather. He was a craftsman." He flicked off an invisible piece of dirt. "It was his last one. He didn't finish it."

Gil couldn't see what was missing.

"I fitted the last planks," Hervé explained. "I painted it and even floated it the year after he died. It had the most perfect balance. You could have hauled anything in it. But wooden boats were already going out of style—my father had a fiberglass one, lighter and faster. After we put this one away for the winter, we didn't take it out again."

Hervé sat on an old stool. Gil glanced at the inflatable floats and flexible swimming noodles.

"Did you use these?"

"My son and niece," Hervé said. "They liked to horse around."

"You don't like to spend time in the water?"

Hervé seemed even more amused than before. "I like the water. But when I was young, I preferred to explore. I know the area better than most anyone else."

A line of horseshoes were nailed on to several planks on

one wall. They seemed out of place in a space dedicated to boats and to water and winter sports.

"Where did these come from?" Gil asked.

"Draft horses," Hervé said, "back in the day when this was a farm. They used to pull the plow, the sleigh, everything you needed. My father liked to collect horseshoes as a boy."

Gil remembered his visits to Sturbridge Village in Massachusetts, where people reenacted the life of early nineteenth-century farmers. "You had to use a blacksmith to fit them, right?"

Hervé blinked. "I suppose. I never really thought about it. It was before my time, you know."

Back in Montreal, Maurice had told him that Enko's ring had been made by a blacksmith in this part of the Laurentians. He had suggested that Gil explore older settlements— like Le Gros-Curé. They had mined garnet nearby.

"Was there a blacksmith in Le Gros-Curé?"

"I would think so," Hervé replied. "Blacksmiths were in every village. You needed them for horses, to fix farm equipment, for all kinds of things."

"How about at the end of the nineteenth century?"

Hervé scratched his head. "It was a small settlement then, but there was probably a blacksmith."

Gil remembered the plaque in French with pictures of settlers. Was one of them a blacksmith? Why hadn't he stayed in the village instead of trying to trek up to L'Annonciation?

"You know," Hervé continued, "I'm no historian. You

should go to the *bibliothèque*. Maybe they have that information."

"Bee-blee-oh-TEK?"

"A place to borrow books."

"A library?"

Hervé grinned. "In French, *une librairie* is where they sell books. I can take you tomorrow."

Gil's knee no longer hurt when Hervé woke him the next morning. He was feeling antsy, ready to leave in case his parents were on their way. But Hervé explained that the *bibliothèque* didn't open until ten. "You can wait at the *quincaillerie*," he said. "I have paperwork to do, and some shelving."

"Can I help?" Gil asked.

Hervé hesitated. "A box of mittens and hats arrived, all jumbled up. I cleared some shelves for them."

"No problem."

"Jumbled up" was an accurate description, as if the shipper had decided to make unpacking as complicated as possible. Gil sorted half a dozen kinds of mittens and gloves and a bunch of hats, child and adult sizes. He didn't notice that Hervé had unlocked the front door until a customer picked up a pair of insulated gloves and asked Gil something in French. Fortunately Hervé approached and answered the question. The woman returned them to the shelf, shaking her head. Hervé never lost his smile.

After the woman left, Hervé turned to Gil. "The

bibliothèque is open now." At the front door, he pointed down the street. "Just up that block. Take a right and it will be the big building on your left. You can't miss it."

The library was a one-story building with a wheelchair ramp on its side. The tiny parking lot next to it was cracked and in obvious need of repair. The concrete steps to the front door were pockmarked, and one was missing a corner. But when Gil entered the building, the well-lit, open space felt as if it were brimming with books.

A patron sat at one of the computers that lined a wall. Gil briefly thought of emailing his parents. He could reassure them that he was okay, maybe lead them off track. But he worried that they'd trace the email to the library. He had come here for one purpose—to find out about blacksmiths in the area. That was what he needed to concentrate on.

A short, stout, middle-aged woman with straight, stringy light brown hair approached. *"Je peux t'aider?"* She had asked if she could help.

"Do you speak English?"

She scrunched her face and raised her hands. *"Un peu. Juste un peu."* A little.

Gil felt more and more embarrassed by his inability to communicate with people in their own tongue. He'd have to improvise.

"May I use one of your computers?" He pointed to the wall.

"Mais oui." She led him to a terminal.

For the next half hour, Gil fruitlessly searched for information about blacksmiths in Le Gros-Curé. He sat back and frowned.

"*Peut-être je peux t'aider,*" the librarian said. She had returned, offering to help again.

Yes, he needed help.

Between pantomimes, scribbles on borrowed paper, the few words of French he understood and the few words of English she knew, he was able to ask whether they had any information about blacksmiths—"*forgerons,*" he pronounced carefully—in this area in the nineteenth century.

The librarian lifted her finger. "*Une minute.*" She went to another terminal and began typing something in. She clicked several times, shook her head, cleared her results and tried again. About five minutes later, she sat back and beckoned to Gil.

"Not very much," she said. "*Mais viens.* Maybe this help."

She took him down an aisle between shelves. She pulled one book out, slipped it back in and then did the same with several more. All the books were in French. How on earth was he going to read whatever she showed him?

She pulled out an old volume, thick, bound in cardboard and beige cloth, with a fraying spine. She opened it to the back, went down the table of contents and stopped midpage. She flipped through the pages and pointed to a heading. "*Voilà!*"

She handed the book to Gil. In bold letters was "*Occupations régionales.*" This appeared to be a census book.

"*Merci!*" he said.

"Ben sûr," she said, grinning. "You are the welcome."

He examined the book at a desk. Although some of the words were the same as in English, nothing made much sense to him. He turned the page and was rewarded with two tables between paragraphs of text. They listed *occupations,* followed by dates in ten-year intervals, from 1875 to 1925. Under each date was the number of people who worked in each profession. Each table was for a different set of towns.

The first occupation on the list was *"cultivateur."* Farmer, Gil figured. Then *"bûcheron," "mécanicien," "médecin"* and more. He found *"forgeron"* about halfway down the list. There were several in 1875. The number stayed almost constant for decades.

He scanned the lines of text again, frustrated by his inability to read. He noticed people's names: Jacques Laramée. Pierre Fléchette. And then, as he was about to give up, he noticed Henri Miller. Hmm. Same last name as Old Man Miller. The paragraph mentioned 1875. He also read place names: La Macaza. Le Gros-Curé. La Minerve. And the name Miller reappeared several times. He checked the words again and saw *"forgeron"* at least once in the paragraph. Yes. Henri Miller. *Forgeron.* In 1875 or thereabouts. Just in this area.

He sat straight in wonder. Could this Henri Miller be related to Old Man Miller on the lake?

He noticed the librarian snap her head back down to her work. She had probably been watching him. On a scrap of paper Gil wrote: "1875. Henri Miller. La Macaza. Le Gros-Curé. La Minerve. Forgeron."

He examined the book some more but couldn't make out anything else useful. He did notice a paragraph that listed a Jean-Baptiste Durocher along with many other names, with *"cultivateur"* appearing frequently. He wrote that down as well. Perhaps Hervé was related.

He returned the book to the librarian. *"Merci,"* he said.

"De rien," she said. "It help?"

He nodded. *"Beaucoup."* A lot.

She smiled. "You are the welcome here. I help again."

15

Escape

Gil recognized the young man at the register when he returned to the *quincaillerie*: he had sold him the ticket to L'Annonciation!

"Well, hello," the man said. "You are back already?"

"Don't you work at the motel?" Gil asked.

Hervé approached from a side aisle. "Jean-François. Gil. You know each other?"

After a minute's confusion, they sorted it out. Jean-François worked part-time at both places, during the late morning and early afternoon at the *quincaillerie* and in the evening at the motel. He seemed genuinely concerned when Hervé told him that Gil had been mugged.

"There's a gang that comes this way from Hull," he said. "They may be part of it. The police probably know about them."

No. Gil wouldn't contact the police. They'd call his

parents—the last thing he needed right now. Luckily Hervé missed Jean-François's hint.

"We're off to lunch," he said. "You're in charge, Jean-François." He tilted his head at Gil and led him through the back to his pickup. "Jean-François is a nephew."

Gil wondered how many other people in town were related to Hervé.

They drove to his house—a twenty-minute trip. "After we eat, I'll head back to the *quincaillerie*," Hervé said. "You'll be okay by yourself?"

"Sure."

Hervé prepared sandwiches and served them on the porch overlooking the lake, taking advantage of the beautiful weather.

"Any luck at the *bibliothèque*?" he asked.

Gil put his sandwich on his plate. "Yeah." He pulled out the paper from his pants pocket and read from it. "Jean-Baptiste Durocher. Are you related to him?"

Hervé lit up. "My great-grandfather. We called him Pépé. He built this house."

"He was listed with other farmers."

Hervé's smile lingered as he chewed. "*Oui*. They were all farmers. And a lot more."

"The book also mentioned *forgerons*." Gil was rather proud of his pronunciation.

"Blacksmiths?" Hervé asked.

Clearly Gil's pronunciation wasn't as good as he thought. He laughed. "*Oui*."

Hervé nodded, pleased. "I told you it would help."

"It mentioned a Henri Miller, back in 1875."

"Really?"

"Do you think he might be related to Old Man Miller?"

"Don't know. Miller is a common name."

Miller? An English name? "Up here?"

"*Ben oui*. Some of the English settled around here, too."

"Do you think we could ask him?" Gil asked.

"Whether he's related?" Hervé scratched the back of his head. "I don't know, Gil. He really likes his privacy. But we can check the *chaloupe* this evening, and if it's ready I can ride you over. I do have some old business with him to discuss."

"That'd be great!"

"Don't expect too much, okay? He's not what you would call the, um, sharing type."

"Just bringing me over would be terrific. Thanks!"

Hervé finished his sandwich. "Time for me to head back."

Gil waved as Hervé drove off. He washed the dishes but couldn't find the dish towel. It was probably being laundered. At home, his mom stored clean ones in a drawer under a back counter. He turned around but saw no counter, just a small desk with Hervé's computer on it. Next to it, though, was a tall set of drawers. Maybe those had towels.

Bingo! He found a small stack of them in the bottom drawer. He straightened, pleased with his deductive reasoning, and noticed the scratch paper next to the computer on which "Marsh" had been written in neat script.

Gil stared at his name, then at the computer.

The screen was black. On a hunch, Gil pressed the power button—yes, the monitor came back to life, the program for the Internet browser still on. Gil checked over his shoulder, though he knew no one else was around, then sat at the desk and clicked on the icon for recent usage. A list appeared. His stomach knotted up at the last entry. "White Pages—Green Valley, Connecticut."

Hervé had been tracking his parents down.

Gil felt as though someone had punched him in the chest. Hervé had betrayed him! He had called his parents even after Gil had told him he didn't want him to. They probably weren't home, but they would be checking their messages, even from wherever they were in Montreal. Hervé had kept Gil busy all morning, working him in the store, sending him to the library, even offering to take him to Old Man Miller's in the evening—to stall him. To let his parents catch up with him.

Well, he wasn't going back home! Not yet, anyway. He hadn't found Enko's ring. He hadn't spoken to the immortal man. He hadn't visited Enko's grave.

What should he do?

He breathed in deep, calming himself, forcing himself to assess the situation. His knee had almost healed, but he knew that if he started running, it'd get worse soon and he'd be a sitting duck. Besides, Hervé probably knew every road and path in this area. He had lived here all his life! And Gil wasn't ready to bushwhack.

He glanced out the window. A lone *chaloupe* with an outboard chugged past, not too far from the shore—the only vessel in sight.

If his parents were on the way, Gil should follow the one

lead he had. Old Man Miller. He'd go now, before Hervé returned, before his parents had a chance to make it up here.

Gil hiked down the hill to the *chaloupe*. Hervé had said that the patching needed to set properly but that it should hold after twenty-four hours. The putty looked almost the same as it did yesterday. Gil tested it with his fingers. It felt hard. He pressed a fingernail into it—no give. It was solid.

He looked around. He'd need the plug.

The shed. He climbed the several feet. Luckily, Hervé hadn't pushed the padlock all the way in. Gil tugged it open and unlatched the door.

As his eyes adjusted to the dimness inside, Gil realized how difficult it was going to be to find anything. The shed was jam-packed with an outboard motor hooked to a board on the wall, a bunch of old tools, countless cans filled with nails, tubes on one shelf, saws hanging on the wall, a line of oil bottles on a shelf, a pickax underneath, ropes coiled on pegs, several sets of oars leaning in the back. The jumble confused him. What did the plug look like? And where did Hervé store it?

He searched the shelves nearest the door, without luck. But he did find screws and bolts in one can and rubber rings in another. He returned to the *chaloupe* and measured the drain—the diameter was exactly the length of his thumbnail. Back at the shed, he rummaged through the cans, fitting bolts and screws together and threading rubber rings with them.

Yes, he thought, this should work.

Back at the *chaloupe,* he threaded one ring with a screw, pushed the screw into the hole, threaded another ring over the end and bolted it down, as tight as he dared without damaging the rubber. The fit wasn't perfect, but the rubber rings would keep the water out—they had to.

He briefly thought about putting the outboard motor on the boat, but quickly dismissed the idea. He had never operated one and wasn't sure how it worked. He grabbed a pair of oars instead. All he had to do now was get the boat into the water.

Fortunately, the shore sloped. Slippery sod lay all the way to the short drop a few feet from the water's edge. Gil gave a shove. The boat slipped off the wooden supports and slid smoothly for several feet. He pushed without much effort and had almost reached the end of the sod when the boat came to a loud, scraping halt.

What had Gil hit?

He circled around, and sure enough, a rough rock jutted out under the front of the boat—a white quartz hidden by weeds. Gil checked for stones farther down and found none. He pivoted the boat off the stone, returned to the stern, straightened the angle and pushed again, but more carefully now. The boat slid off the sod and tipped onto the sand.

Gil took off his shoes, threw them into the boat along with the oars and rolled up his jeans. The water gave him a cold jolt at first, but he quickly got used to the temperature. He pulled the boat into the lake, grabbed the rope at the bow and tied it to the pier. Then he checked the plug. It held: no water seeped through, as far as he could tell. He had done it. He had floated the boat!

What else did he need? He returned to the house.

Gil felt guilty rummaging through Hervé's drawers. But the man had tracked down his parents—he had probably spoken to them already! And they were probably on their way here right now. He had to leave immediately.

He found a big flashlight and a few slices of bread, which he stuffed into a sack he found in a closet. He grabbed his toothbrush and acetaminophen. He didn't know when he would return.

Gil was no thief. He'd pay Hervé back, he vowed, once this was all over. Right now, he needed to get some questions answered. But he hesitated and scratched out a note on the pad. "I'll bring back your things. I promise." He left it next to the computer.

He stowed the sack next to his sneakers in the bow, undid the mooring and pushed off. He hoped Hervé would understand.

16
Crossing the lake

The breeze blew stronger on the lake. Fortunately, it came from the north and pushed the *chaloupe* along.

Although Hervé had been vague about Miller's location, Gil understood he needed to head toward the western shore. If he kept close to it, he hoped to find the man's house. Gil rowed across the main channel, drifting southward. He hadn't realized how wide the lake was. For a fleeting moment he wondered whether he should have brought a life jacket. He was a strong swimmer, but he didn't know if he'd make it to shore if he fell in.

He took off his shirt, letting the sun warm his back and the breeze wick away some of the sweat he had built up from rowing. Well, if he did end up in the water, he might cool off.

He wheeled the boat around to survey the land. Shallow bays and small peninsulas wove in and out. He rowed south and passed two small islands. The lakeside cottages and piers disappeared. The lake channel narrowed dramatically, and a thick forest of pine, birch and maple crowded both shores. Skeletons of trees, mostly submerged and surrounded by lily pads, populated the tiny coves at the water's edge.

A bird surfaced behind the *chaloupe,* just a few boat lengths away, startling Gil. A loon! He'd only seen them in photographs. Where had it come from? He paused, oars in the air, watching the bird float placidly. Then, in an instant, it dove underwater and was gone. Gil stared at the spot, expecting it to resurface at any moment, but as the seconds ticked by to a minute, the bird didn't reappear. His puzzlement was cut short by a thump and a scrape on one side of the boat. He looked into the water, and the boat, which had continued on its own momentum, floated past a submerged log sticking straight up, its sawed end only a few inches from the surface. The water around it was deep enough so that Gil couldn't see the bottom.

He shivered. What else did the lake hide?

He maneuvered a little farther from shore and turned his head every few strokes, checking the water for other possible dangers. He saw a bright red *"Privé"* sign on a tree at the water's edge. Private property. The shore curved around, leading to a deep hidden bay. Gil realized that he had been following one side of a long peninsula. Past it, the lake widened again. He could see it continuing farther south, past several more islands, without any signs of habitation.

This must be Old Man Miller's domain. But where was he going to find him?

He floated for a minute more, then heard an eerie cry—

a cross between a laugh and a yell—coming from deep within the peninsula's bay. That was his signal. He aimed the boat toward the source of the cry and started rowing. He slowed as he entered the bay, intimidated by the looming trees and dead trunks poking into the lake.

The cry repeated.

He swiveled around. Two loons floated only yards away. One of them had uttered that freaky cry—he was sure. They were so close he could see the black-and-white speckles on their backs and the collars below their black heads. Fascinated by the birds, he almost missed the glint of sunlight reflected from something among the trees on the peninsula.

He only noticed after he floated past, and the glint had disappeared. Had he imagined it? He rowed in the opposite direction, peering into the forest.

Nothing. But something had been there, he was sure.

He decided to risk downed trees and brought the *chaloupe* closer to shore, checking the water carefully after each stroke. A sandy spot opened up near some flat rocks that sloped up from the water's edge. The trees grew a little farther back. There was no pier nor any evidence of a boat, but the spot looked perfect for docking. He rowed in.

The *chaloupe*'s front end scraped on the sand. Gil climbed out and lifted the boat, so that almost half of it lay on sloping land, then wrapped the mooring line around a sapling. He slipped on his shirt and shoes but decided against taking the sack. Gil didn't plan on exploring very far—just enough to see if he hadn't imagined the glint.

He saw the cabin as soon as he entered the trees.

Dark brown, with the roof lower than the trees surrounding it, it blended in perfectly with the forest. The sunlight reflected off the water and gave a dappled light along the side of the house, as if the wood were decorated with shimmering yellow leopard spots. Gil noticed the small window on the side—one of the dapples must have reflected off of it.

Was this Old Man Miller's place?

He thought perhaps he should call out, to see if anyone was there. He took a step toward the cabin. The barrel of a rifle darted out from behind a tree and aimed for his head.

"*Bouge pas!*"

The voice was deep, gravelly and quiet, as if it didn't get used much.

Gil froze, terror seizing him. What had he said?

The man circled around, the rifle tip inches from Gil's face. He was taller than Gil, but not by much. He had black wiry hair and a bushy beard. His eyes were almost colorless—a gray that seemed to reflect the forest around him—and set deep within layers of creases. They narrowed as he appraised Gil.

"*Un jeune!*"

Gil blinked and tried to swallow. What did the man say?

"*Qui es-tu?*" the man asked.

Gil recognized the tone—a question.

"I . . . I don't speak . . ."

The man scowled. He lowered the rifle a bit. It was still aimed at Gil, but the man had relaxed his shoulders.

"American?"

Gil nodded slightly.

"Go home," the man said.

He aimed the tip down, away from Gil. His accent had a Scottish lilt, without a hint of French.

"Are you Mr. Miller?" Gil asked.

Faster than Gil thought possible, the rifle tip was back up by his head.

"I said, go home!"

Gil didn't have a choice. He backed up slowly and stumbled over a branch. He turned slightly to see where he was going. Miller—given the man's reaction, Gil was positive of his identity—didn't move. The rifle remained aimed at Gil's head. Gil didn't think that this man would miss.

He had to turn around completely when he reached the shore—so he moved quickly. He launched the *chaloupe,* badly scraping the bottom, and clambered in. He was too afraid to remove his sneakers, and they were now soaked. He looked into the trees as he placed the oars into the locks. Miller was invisible, but Gil knew that the rifle was still aimed at him.

He rowed out of the deep bay, around the tip of the wide peninsula, and was level with the *"Privé"* sign. Old Man Miller must have put it up. Gil worried that the man might follow him on land to make sure he had left. But the thick bushes didn't move, and there was no sign of a person anywhere.

He blew his breath out, realizing for the first time how tight he felt—fear gripping him. He shook out his legs and noticed the puddle at the bottom of the boat. He had brought in water with him when he had launched from Miller's property, but not that much. He looked behind him—there was a glistening near the putty, which formed a thin line down the boat bottom and under his bench. The various scrapes must have loosened the patching that Hervé had placed on the bottom.

He looked at the plug. It still seemed watertight, but he wasn't certain. Was that wetness around the rubbering? It did look slightly askew.

Gil didn't fear sinking, not yet. The leaks were too slow. But they were likely to get worse. He needed to dock, preferably with the hull out of the water. What were his options?

He couldn't return to Hervé. Not with his parents on their way. And Miller had made it clear he didn't want him.

Maybe Miller would have been friendlier if Gil had announced himself instead of sneaking up the way he had. He should return. Plan something to say. Get on his good side. Turn on the old charm.

Yes. Gil could manage that. But he needed to think it through. He knew nothing about the man. Maybe if he scoped out Miller's property quietly, he'd be able to figure out the best approach. Miller's cabin was on the other side of the peninsula. What if Gil docked the *chaloupe* on this side and walked across? Miller wouldn't expect that.

The shore was as unwelcoming as before, but Gil was paying closer attention. One of the smaller inlets showed some promise. It had a little space between the dead trees. He maneuvered around underwater branches still attached to downed trunks, and aimed for a channel between an enormous tree skeleton and a desiccated pine. He briefly wondered what had damaged all these trees, then became tangled in branches.

The water looked dark, but he was so close to shore, it couldn't be too deep. Gil stood in the *chaloupe* and grabbed the nearby tree skeleton. It didn't move—it felt as if it were set in cement. The part of the trunk above water was dry, gray, and speckled with moss. Gil leaned over and pushed with both hands, putting as much weight as he dared into the push. A few bubbles popped upward from the muck at the bottom—which, Gil now realized, lay only a few inches away—but the tree didn't give.

Emboldened, he held on to a thick vertical branch and stepped onto the tree trunk. Many more bubbles came up, but the trunk didn't sink.

Now that he was out of the *chaloupe,* it floated higher. He pushed it forward hard between the trunks, as far as it would go. The boat lurched, and the bow rose, sliding onto branches.

Gil was pretty sure that the boat was secure, but as a precaution, he plunged one of the oars down hard into the muck behind the boat, its handle sticking out. Gil hoped it would act as a backstop, preventing the boat from moving backward. To Gil's surprise, the oar went very deep: only a few inches stuck above the waterline. How deep was this mud? When he tried to readjust the oar, the mud grabbed it hard. Yes. This was the perfect anchor. Gil plunged the second oar next to the first. Now the boat wasn't going anywhere.

He grabbed his bag and crept along the log, from branch to branch. It curved upward to where the roots must have been, right by the water's edge. There was only a foot and a half of muck between him and the tall grass. He leapt.

His right foot landed on sand. A pain shot through his healing knee. His left foot landed in the mud. As he lifted it up, the muck nabbed his sneaker, leaving him shoeless on one side.

Gil cursed and turned. With some effort, he pried his shoe loose—it was now covered in black slime and stank of old rot.

Well, he had no choice. He'd have to walk around with what he had.

But he had made it to shore. He climbed through the prickly branches of a bush to a forest jumble. Old pines with sharp branches grew next to the occasional ancient birch or maple. The trees weren't that close together, but the ground was uneven and covered by limbs, unexpected rocks, rotting logs and holes that Gil discovered only by stepping into them. He tripped several times before he thought to use a dead branch to probe the ground.

He tried to orient himself toward the cabin. The land dipped and rose ahead of him. As he climbed the small rise, he smelled smoke. Wood smoke. Old Man Miller's cabin must be closer than he had realized. What direction did the smoke come from?

He closed his eyes and pivoted around, trying to decide where the smoke smelled the strongest. There! He reopened his eyes and squinted through the trees. The forest angled down very gently, and farther off, a line of pines grew close together. They looked as if they had been planted. He headed toward the line as quietly as he could.

Gil reached a long wall of firewood stacked neatly next to the pines, under a series of makeshift lean-tos. Gil held his breath. He had reached Miller's cabin.

Two paths wound down—one to the back of the cabin just below, and the other to a low brick wall embedded into a rock-and-earth mound with a metal chimney rising from its center, smoke curling up. Miller stood by the metal door in the mound and was peering in.

Gil shrunk back. What was the man doing? Miller straightened, clanged the door shut and headed back to his cabin by another path that connected it to the mound. Gil noticed a large shed partially hidden by the mound, also sporting a chimney.

He heard a door from the cabin open and shut. He kept still a little longer, wondering whether Miller was going to come back out, and the unmistakable odor of baking bread wafted up.

Gil's mouth watered. He couldn't help it. But where was the smell coming from?

He glanced at the mound and the shed, and curiosity took over. Slowly, carefully, he climbed down. He made no noise—he was sure of it. He reached the metal door in the mound and stopped. The door was at waist level and just big enough to fit a person's torso if he leaned in. It looked like the opening for a pizza oven, only bigger. As if to confirm his suspicions, a wooden paddle with a long handle leaned up against the brickwork. This was where the bread was being baked!

But now Gil was distracted by the shed next to the mound.

The door, the size of a garage door, had been left open, and Gil could see inside. An open fireplace lay under a huge inverted funnel chimney that filled the back wall. An anvil stood a few feet away. One wall was lined with hammers of every size, large tongs, several bellows, some tools Gil didn't recognize and two leather aprons. A large vise was attached to a low bench near the anvil.

A smithy! Why had Old Man Miller built a smithy in the middle of the forest? It looked well used. The floor had been swept. The fireplace had ash and recently burned wood. A hammer lay on the bench.

Gil's mind raced. Had Henri Miller, the 1875 blacksmith, passed on his craft to his family?

Gil thought he heard a creak but wasn't sure. He needed to move out of sight. He crept around the mound to another set of lean-tos, under which were piled more cords of firewood. Miller sure burned a lot. How did he get all this wood here?

Another clang made Gil jump. The noise came from the oven door. Old Man Miller must have returned. Gil scrambled behind one of the lean-tos that backed into the forest. He wasn't ready to confront Miller, not yet. He hadn't figured out what he was going to say.

He heard a snap, like a footstep on a branch, close now. Gil slunk backward, turned to run and tripped over a rock. He landed on his right knee, causing pain to shoot through it. When he tried to stand, his leg buckled. He had reinjured himself!

Maybe it was just the shock of the fall, he thought. If he allowed himself a minute, the stabbing pain would ease and he could get out of here. Lying on his side, he cradled his knee, wincing in agony.

"Pretty stupid," a deep voice said.

Miller stood a few paces away with his rifle loose in his hands, the barrel pointing to the ground.

17
Loaves of bread

Gil sat up slowly, dizzy with pain. His knee felt worse than when he had injured it the first time.

Miller didn't move. What was he waiting for? He had his rifle. Was he going to shoot? He didn't look as if he was. That gave Gil hope.

"I'm hurt," Gil said.

"I can see that."

Gil swallowed. "Can you help me?"

"Why should I?"

Gil had no answer. He was a trespasser. Miller had told him to leave. Had threatened to kill him. He seemed to be tightening his grip on the rifle's handle.

Fear washed over Gil in a great tide. He shivered in pain. For the first time since he was a little boy, he struggled not to cry.

Miller turned and, after a few paces, stopped. "When you get to the house, I'll have a poultice ready."

He walked away. Gone.

Gil wasn't sure how long he sat there breathing hard, but Miller didn't return. The man had promised help. Could Gil trust him? He could have shot him, right then and there, but he hadn't. Gil looked round. The boat was too far away. What choice did he have? He concentrated and began a slow crawl to the cabin.

Gil used his arms and good leg to carry his weight, but he couldn't keep his bad knee up for long. He stopped frequently, resting on his side or back, until the pain subsided again. Eventually he reached the stairs at the side of the cabin. They climbed to a door.

The main part of the building had been built over cement blocks. A porch wrapped around the front and sides, and the roof sloped over it. The top half of the cabin was made of hand-hewed logs. A metal chimney pipe poked out of the roof.

Gil sat on the bottom step and pushed his way up, one step at a time, till he reached the porch.

"Round front," Miller said.

A covered wood box sat on one side of the door, and firewood was stacked on the other, all along the porch wall. Gil crawled past the wood. Miller sat on the front porch in an armchair, also made of hewed logs. Next to him was the chair's twin, and behind that the rifle, propped under a grimy window. Gil noticed a second door beyond the window.

Miller pointed to the empty chair. "Sit here."

Gil crawled over and pulled himself up with his arms. He swiveled to sit, and lowered his bad leg with a wince.

Miller handed him a rusty coffee can. "The poultice will help."

The can contained a grayish-green murky substance. Gil touched it with the tip of a finger—it had the consistency of Vaseline and smelled like rotting fish, pungent and awful. He crumpled his nose.

Miller shrugged. "It's up to you. But you have to leave here by sundown. And it's easier to walk than to crawl."

Gil glanced back down at the can, then at Miller. "I can't roll my pants up high enough."

Miller grinned, showing off yellowed, crooked teeth. "I won't jump you."

Embarrassed, Gil shimmied off his pants, which was tricky since he didn't dare stand or put any weight on his bad leg. His knee was swollen and red. A black patch was starting to form where he had hit it. He straightened it slowly and tried to rotate it gently. Everything moved okay, though it hurt.

He frowned in disgust at the tin, but took some ointment with the tips of his fingers and spread it on his knee.

"Work it in," Miller said.

Gil glanced at the man. Miller was staring into the woods out front.

Gingerly at first, then with more vigor, Gil began massaging the greasy ointment in. It started off feeling cool, almost sharp, the coolness seeping into the inflammation and dulling the pain. Then, as he massaged, the coolness warmed until it felt as if intense heat were being applied to his knee. Quickly that sensation faded, too, replaced by an odd but not unpleasant tingling. The pain had disappeared, although the knee remained swollen.

"Wrap it in this," Miller said. He placed a threadbare but clean rag on Gil's armrest.

Gil carefully wrapped the rag around his knee. He tucked the corners into the wrapping and reached for his pants.

"Wait," Miller said. "It needs an hour to set."

Gil had just wrapped the ointment in a cloth. What difference did another layer of cloth make? But he wasn't prepared to argue with Miller, especially since the ointment seemed to be working.

"Thank you," Gil said.

Miller's only acknowledgment was a glance before he returned his gaze to the woods.

They sat in silence for a few minutes. Gil simply didn't know what to say. He was well aware of the rifle within Miller's reach. The pain and the crawl to the cabin had exhausted him. He shut his eyes to think about what he should do next. He didn't expect to fall asleep.

He woke with his head leaning on his shoulder. He straightened with a jolt. Shadows swept across the property, sunlight slanting through. Several loaves of bread cooled on a bench near the front door. How long had he slept? Miller and his rifle were no longer on the porch. Gil reached down for his pants. To his surprise, not a twinge came from his knee as he dressed himself, although he did avoid placing weight on his leg.

He had just zipped up when Miller came up the stairs. He carried two more loaves. He paused, as if to assess how trustworthy Gil might be, and placed one loaf on the porch railing. Then he sat, broke off a piece from the second loaf and handed it to Gil.

Gil stared at the piece for a second. Miller tilted his head only slightly, but enough for Gil to understand that he should sit and eat. The bread was still warm, almost hot. It must have come out of the oven a few minutes ago. Gil devoured it.

"Thank you," Gil said.

Miller nodded and gave him another large chunk, which Gil managed to eat without wolfing it down. Miller then handed over a mug that had been next to his chair.

"Coffee," he said.

The liquid was black, but Gil didn't dare ask for milk or sugar. He took a sip. It tasted lukewarm, bitter and very strong. He drank it all.

"Thank you," he said again.

Miller waved it away. "You've gone to a lot of trouble, for a *jeune*."

Gil stared at the empty coffee mug. "What's a 'juhn'?"

Miller snorted. "A kid."

Gil straightened, stung. Hervé had called him a man.

"You're American, too."

Gil nodded. Miller settled back, tore another hunk of bread from the loaf and began chewing it.

"How . . ." Gil paused, wondering whether Miller would answer his question. But the man just kept chewing, eyes forward. If he didn't want questions, he'd tell Gil. "How did you know I'm from the U.S.?"

"Your accent."

His accent? Gil didn't have an accent! If anyone had an accent, Miller did.

But Miller hadn't finished. "Your shoes. The way you hold yourself, as if you owned the bloody world. Your clothes that belong in a city. Your hair. Your face."

Miller took another bite and chewed.

"But Canadians . . . ?"

"Would know enough French to get by."

Gil had no answer to that.

Miller leaned forward. "So. What's a *jeune américain* doing here, looking for Old Man Miller?"

Gil stared at the cup again. What *was* he doing here? "I thought . . ." He hesitated. "I thought you might be able to help me."

The man showed no surprise. "Was that Durocher's idea?"

Gil started. How did Miller know about Hervé? Miller's face remained impassive as he waited for Gil's answer.

"He said . . . he said he might introduce us."

"But you were too impatient to wait." He bit into his bread.

Gil stared at his hands. This was not going well. But Miller seemed more amused than angry. When the old man finished chewing, he paused. Gil realized that he had an opening now.

"Are you a blacksmith?"

Miller shrugged. "Used to be. Not much call for it now."

"Was your father one, too?" Miller scowled, and Gil realized his mistake. "I mean, I've been trying to find out about blacksmiths from about a hundred years ago, and there was a Miller listed as one around these parts back then. . . ."

Miller sighed. "I see." Then his eyes focused away. His face lost all expression. His jaw relaxed into complete stillness. He sat, immobile, as seconds ticked to a minute. Gil was too afraid to say a word.

Slowly, like a tortoise Gil had once seen at the zoo, Miller swung his head around. His gray eyes focused on Gil. Trapped in Miller's gaze, Gil held his breath. It felt as if Miller were reading him, probing him. Gil was frightened, but he didn't look away. Gil needed answers. He hadn't come all this way to back down.

Gil almost missed Miller's soft answer. "I know about blacksmiths."

Gil allowed himself to breathe. Miller kept staring.

"Did any—" Gil groped for the right words. "Did any make jewelry?"

That made Miller's eyebrows rise. "One or two."

"I have—" Gil began. Then he corrected himself. "I had a ring." A lump formed in his throat, but he ignored it. Miller nodded, expecting more. "It had a garnet in it, dark red, almost black, faceted, perfectly round but flattened, about half the size of a dime." Miller's fixed attention was unnerving. But Gil pressed on. "It was set in silver with six prongs.

Someone told me it had been made about one hundred years ago, probably by a blacksmith in this area."

"One hundred and twenty."

Gil didn't understand the response. "One hundred and twenty?"

"Henri Miller set that stone one hundred and twenty years ago."

"How . . . ? How . . . ?" Gil couldn't come up with the words. How did he know which stone? Which ring? Which date?

Miller looked away, releasing Gil from his gaze. Gil stood, out of breath, and leaned on the railing, facing out. He breathed in through his nose, exhaled through his mouth, and let his heartbeat slow. He felt as if he had run up and down Overhang Rock at full speed.

"How," he said to the trees before him, "how do you know about the ring?"

Miller didn't answer. He picked up the loaf next to Gil, placed it on the bench with the others and went inside. Gil waited. A few minutes later Miller reappeared. He stood before Gil and showed him a cupped hand. Dwarfed by the callused dark brown palm sat the ring—Enko's ring!

Gil felt elation sweep through him, flushing his face. He reached over to take it, and Miller closed his fist.

"But . . ."

Miller shook his head and brought his hand down. "It's not yours anymore."

18
The immortal man

"But they stole it!" Gil couldn't believe it. He had just finished telling Miller what had happened, how the thugs had mugged him, yet nothing he said moved the man. "They attacked me!"

Miller still shook his head. "It was a fair trade. I made a new mudguard; they paid me with a ring."

Gil spat out his next words. "I thought you weren't a blacksmith anymore."

"Not much call for it."

His responses were infuriating.

"But how did they get here? You're cut off—"

At first, Gil didn't recognize Miller's growl as laughter.

"The road's at the bottom of the bay. If you had kept walking instead of knocking yourself over, you'd have run into it."

Gil whirled, slamming his fists onto the porch railing. The man thought he was laughable.

"The ring was a gift!" he yelled. "To me!"

Miller shrugged. "A stone. Set in poor silver. That's all it is."

"It was from someone I loved!" Gil yelled louder.

Miller looked him up and down. "She'll get you something else."

Miller's smirk crowded everything out from Gil's vision. Damn the man! Gil lunged, swinging.

Miller caught Gil's fist and held it in midair. Then he leaned forward without any evident effort. Gil stumbled. Although he felt no pain in his knee, the sharp pressure on his arm and shoulder forced him to step back. Gil pulled his fist to his chest, clasping it with his other hand. Miller squared off—more than ready, it seemed, to take Gil on.

"It's *he*," Gil said between his teeth. "And he's dead."

"That isn't my fault."

Gil raised his other fist. A chipmunk whistled shrilly from one of the trees. Gil began to shake.

And at that moment, Gil saw himself as if from a distance, standing on the porch, one arm up, facing Miller. The old man crouched slightly, ready to fight. To defend himself. Against someone he had doctored and fed.

It dawned on Gil. He had just attacked Old Man Miller! The *one* man on this sorry, misbegotten trip who had the answers he needed.

Before Gil knew what he was doing, he threw his head

backward and screamed. Wave after wave of bottled-up pain, anger and frustration rushed and tumbled through him. He clenched his arms. He arched his back. And when he couldn't breathe anymore, the long, ragged yell subsided.

Gil dropped his arms and took a great, shuddering breath. Then, one breath at a time, he steadied himself. He couldn't look Miller in the eye.

His voice cracked when he spoke next. "I'm sorry."

Miller's shoulders relaxed. Despite everything, he didn't appear angry—almost as if he had expected the outburst. And now he waited for Gil to say more.

"Can you . . ." Gil swallowed. "Can you at least tell me something about it? About the ring?"

Miller didn't answer right away. He stood straighter, appraising the boy. The chipmunk in the tree trilled. Another chipmunk across the way replied. Miller took a step forward.

Gil flinched.

Slowly, Miller brought the ring up so Gil could see the stone up close. "Garnet. You'll find it in a tapped vein a few kilometers from Le Gros-Curé. This one was polished. Someone thought it was beautiful."

"It is," Gil said in his strangled voice.

The stone's color was so deep, the red almost hidden in blackness, it made it both warm and mysterious. Yet it shone as well, reflecting the light.

Miller pointed to the band. "The silver isn't very pure—you can see by the black streaks. It came from someone's spoon, brought from France with the early settlers."

Gil blinked. How did Miller know this?

The man seemed far away. "The ring was meant as a gift—for a young woman."

Gil swallowed again. He was afraid to move, lest he interrupt. Little by little Miller retold the story of Antoine and Clotilde. As he warmed to the tale, he rocked almost imperceptibly. He recounted their courtship and her untimely death, adding details Gil had not heard before. Through Miller, he saw the rough and beautiful land gouged by European axes and plows; he smelled the dirt and manure of the settlers' farms; he heard the bangs of the small hammer the blacksmith used to form the slim silver rod into a ring.

"Antoine Larivière was too young," Miller said. "Lost love makes young men do foolish things."

And Gil heard the thunder of the logs tearing down a swollen river, destroying anything in their path.

"I thought it was a legend," Gil said.

"It has become one," Miller said.

Gil let that sink in. A breeze rustled the leaves overhead.

"Do you know the Labette family?" Gil asked.

Gil thought he saw a flicker in Miller's eyes, as though Gil had finally given him some sort of confirmation.

"Yes. I know of them."

"How did they get the ring?"

Miller paused, appearing to weigh what he should say next. And then he told him.

When Antoine Larivière left for the lumber camps, his father expected the worst. When they brought his son's body home for the funeral, M. Larivière didn't cry. His heart had broken months before, and he saved his strength to care for his family. After the undertaker returned the ring, M. Larivière walked through the spring mud to the smithy.

"I don't want this."

The blacksmith was perplexed. "I have no use for a ring."

"It brings bad luck. Get rid of it."

"I can melt it down. Make you a new spoon."

"No. Bad luck will taint the silver."

The smith scratched his bushy beard. "I can at least return the stone."

M. Larivière refused. The smith placed the ring on a high shelf across from the forge.

A few weeks later, a young man appeared, heading north with a wagon full of supplies for sale. He needed his cart horse shod. As the man held the docile beast's head, the smith worked on one hoof at a time. The man noticed the garnet that reflected the red light from the forge.

"That a precious stone?" he asked.

The smith put the hoof down to fetch the ring. "It's garnet. I set it for a pair of lovers, but they both died."

The young man examined it. "That's poor silver."

The smith grinned. "I'll trade stone and silver for a good pot."

The young man agreed. "It'll bring me fortune, I predict."

The blacksmith waved goodbye when the young man headed north. The printing on the clapboard of the peddler wagon read "Léopold Labette."

"Do you know what happened to the peddler after he left?"

Miller smiled now, wrinkles crowding around his eyes and nose. "He did very well, I heard, over by James Bay—a merchant in a godforsaken country. He found a wife, grew a family and staked some land. His heirs cashed in when the province built the dam."

"Dam?"

"Hydroelectric," Miller said. "The province bought up a bunch of land. By then the Labette clan had moved south, but the family still owned thousands of acres."

James Bay! That was on Hudson Bay, even farther north. Could Enko have been buried there? Miller must have read his mind.

"It's flooded now. You won't find anything underwater."

Gil stared at Miller, unsure if he understood. "You mean there's nothing there—nothing of the Labettes'?"

"Nothing," Miller said.

"How do you know?"

"It's what I've heard. And I've heard a lot." He gave Gil a glance. "You knew the young Labette, the one who died in the States."

Gil nodded, unable to say more.

"That was a tragedy," Miller said.

Gil let himself sink into one of the chairs. Miller sat next to him and placed the ring on his armrest, within reach of them both.

"You were the blacksmith, weren't you?" Gil said.

"*Oui.*"

Miller said it quietly, but to Gil, it sounded like a thunderclap, one that reverberated down his spine. He sat next to an immortal man.

"How did you live so long?"

Miller now grinned in earnest. "By not asking that question."

"But . . ."

Miller became serious. "It is the only answer I have. It is how I am. I don't think about it anymore."

"There must be something that you do, or eat—"

Miller scowled. "There is nothing." He sighed deeply, as if he were trying to rid himself of a memory. "I am not heartless, Gil. I nurse wounds and heal sicknesses. Yet every single person I have ever helped has died eventually, no matter what I did."

"You can't . . . bring back the dead?"

Miller shut his eyes. "No." He paused. "Lord knows how much I wish I could."

Gil wondered how many people Miller had watched die; how many of those he had cared about, maybe even loved. And suddenly, he felt sorry for this old man who lived by himself.

"Maybe there's something about your DNA—"

Miller waved a hand. "I am not a lab rat to be poked at. I live here. I bother no one. And no one bothers me." He gave Gil a sideways glance. "Unless they're foolish."

They sat in silence for a while longer. Looking through the trees, Gil could see the lake. Ripples of light reflected up, and the water's edge glowed a bright green, contrasting with the deep greens and browns within the woods.

"Did you ever think of living somewhere else?" Gil asked.

"This isn't my first home. Nor my grandest. But it suits me."

How many places had Miller lived? But Gil could tell that the time for questions was over. Miller had risen, pocketed the ring and begun gathering the cooled loaves on the bench.

Gil rose, too.

Miller eyed him. "You can rest."

Gil stood straight. "You fixed my knee, and fed me, and told me what I wanted to know."

"So you're ready to go." Miller seemed to approve.

"No. I'm ready to work." Gil owed the man at least this much.

For the first time, Miller looked puzzled.

"Tell me what to do," Gil said.

Miller raised an eyebrow. "Can you stack wood?"

Miller had him carry armloads of firewood from one of the lean-tos and stack it along the side wall, as high as Gil could reach.

When he finished, Miller fed him some more bread with slices of a hard, cheddar-like cheese, and another mug of the bitter coffee. Gil consumed it all gratefully.

"Now it's time for you to go," Miller said.

The sun had already begun slipping behind the western hills. Gil stared at his feet. "Couldn't I stay? I'd help you. I'm strong and a fast learner."

Miller scowled. "No. You don't belong here. You're soft and young. And I don't want company."

The reply stung. Hadn't Gil proved his worth? "But—"

Miller's eyebrows lowered farther. "No. Leave. I gave you hospitality. Don't make me regret it." The man stood by the stairs, immobile, his utter stillness as threatening as the rifle he had held to Gil's head.

Gil knew there was no point arguing. He put on the jacket he had removed to stack wood, and found his sack next to one of the chairs. He walked past Miller, silently seething. Why was the man so stubborn?

When Gil reached the lean-tos he had encountered on his way to the cabin, he felt a tap on his shoulder. He jumped.

Miller stood next to him. Gil hadn't heard him follow.

"Don't leave mad, young man," Miller said. "You have lost someone you love, but you don't have to be a fool." He took Gil's hand and placed the ring in it. "It is neither good luck nor ill omen. It's a stone set in poor silver. Remember that."

Gil couldn't answer. His throat seemed to have closed up.

Miller pointed between two trees. "If you follow that deer track, you'll come to a clearing. Then head east. Durocher's boat is still there."

Gil glanced down at the garnet, amazed that it was his again, and slipped it onto his finger. He coughed once. "Thank you."

Miller turned, walked down the bend by his cabin and was gone, as if Gil had imagined him all along.

19

sunk

The sun was truly setting when Gil reached the boat. He had to struggle to remove the oars he had driven into the muck. When they came up, they were covered in stinky black slime.

It also took him more effort than he had planned to pull the boat out. He almost lost his balance a half dozen times, tugging and pushing. He scraped the bottom hard when he finally pried it loose, but he didn't slow down. He wanted to be on his way before dark. He kept an eye on the opposite shore: the trees still reflected pink light from the sunset.

With relief, he launched himself out of the cove.

He had a surprising amount of energy and rowed with steady, quick motions. He passed the two islands that marked the end of Old Man Miller's territory, and decided to cross to the eastern shore while there was still enough light for him to be visible—he feared getting hit by a speedboat in the darkness. He propped the flashlight on the seat next to him as a beacon, glad that he had thought to bring it.

The wind had died down, and he didn't drift. He was about halfway across when he noticed how wet his feet were getting. Almost two inches of water filled the bottom. All the scraping must have further damaged the bottom of the boat. The plug no longer covered the drain completely. The leaks had sped up.

He redoubled his efforts. He couldn't swim back to Hervé's, not from here. By the time he neared the opposite shore, the water had risen by another inch, he was sure. The boat slowed, too, with all the extra weight. Gil kept rowing. He had another half a mile—three-quarters at the most.

But the water seemed to rise faster. A large speedboat whizzed by, and its wake threatened to swamp the boat. Gil lost precious time holding on to the gunnels, desperately trying to steady his sinking vessel.

He avoided a rocky outcrop and headed closer to shore, but the water inside the boat lapped at his bench. He didn't have a choice. He aimed for the tiny beach in the cove beyond the outcrop. Thirty feet from shore, the boat sank.

The aluminum vessel drifted down slowly but steadily. Gil tried to swim away but his sneaker snagged on the oarlock. The boat began to drag him under! Gil thrashed furiously. The sneaker yanked loose. But still Gil had trouble keeping himself afloat. His clothes had become waterlogged and weighed him down. Panic mounted. Gil kicked off his sneakers. He peeled off his jacket. Pulled off his pants. He abandoned them to the lake. Coughing and sputtering, his pulse pounding in his ears, he swam to shore.

Gil stumbled onto the sand and rolled onto his back. He gulped air. His heart thumped in his chest. He needed to calm down, but he also knew he couldn't rest here for long. Night was falling, the temperature was dropping quickly, his shirt and underwear were soaked through and he was cold. He sat up. The beach fronted a tiny cabin on stilts. The road must be behind it. He stood—a little shaky still, but he could walk the rest of the way. He ran his fingers through his hair. The ring snagged.

What?

He untangled it, took it off his finger and stared. The stone was missing. At least two of the prongs were broken.

No. His chest clenched. No! This couldn't be.

He dropped onto all fours and searched the sand. Light was failing, but Gil used the tips of his fingers, touching every square inch in larger and larger concentric circles.

He didn't find the stone.

It had to be here. All this effort, only to lose his final link to Enko?

He stared at the lake. Maybe it was by the waterline, buried under the gently moving sand. He needed to dig. Starting at one end, inch by inch, he sifted the sand along the small shoreline. But his efforts were fruitless. He couldn't find it anywhere. He went deeper. The sand turned to muck. The bottom sloped rapidly.

By now the sky had filled with stars, and a light breeze

blew in. Gil straightened and shivered, knee-deep in the lake. Somewhere, somewhere in that black water, he had lost the stone—probably when he had yanked off his jeans or struggled out of his jacket.

"NO!"

The scream echoed. "No-o-o-o-o." A second of silence followed the echo's fade, and a loon cried in the distance. It sounded like maniacal laughter.

Gil had lost everything. Enko. The garnet. Hervé's boat. His own clothes. He hugged himself, fresh pain stabbing at his chest, struggled to shore and sank to his knees.

"No, no, no, no, no. . . ."

He curled into a ball and let the sobs overtake him.

20
Homecoming

Gil had reached the end of his road. He had no idea how long he spent on the beach, but the cold bit him. He needed to find shelter. Hervé's house was only a quarter mile away. Gil plodded there, barefoot and shivering. An SUV was parked next to Hervé's truck. His parents had arrived. He was too numb to care.

His mother folded her arms around him, but he stood immobile, like a statue.

Hervé tried to bottle his anger, but it remained palpable. "You sank my *chaloupe*? You lost my best flashlight?"

Gil hung his head, staring down at his cut-up feet. "I'll repay you. I promise."

His father looked grim. "I'll make sure he keeps that promise."

They bundled him into the rented car and took him to the

hotel across the street from the *quincaillerie,* where he shared a room with his parents.

"I'm sorry, Gil," his mother said. "We have to keep an eye on you."

The next few days passed in a blur. Gil's mind was stuck on the beach, searching for the stone, while they purchased clothes for him and drove to the U.S. consulate in Montreal to get him the necessary paperwork to return home. His parents pressed him with questions, only some of which he was able to answer.

When he told them how he had lost all his money to Adèle, his father was furious. "You sure you can't find that girl? We'll call the police."

"Do you know how many Québécois are called Adèle?"

His father fumed, but his mother calmed him.

"Let Gil pull himself together first."

The next morning, over breakfast, his mother told him she had spoken to Enko's mother.

"She told you where to find Enko's grave," Gil said.

Mom nodded.

Gil put down his fork. His stomach fluttered angrily. "Will you take me?" His voice cracked.

"Your paperwork will be ready this afternoon," his father said. It sounded like a discouraging warning.

His mother glanced at his father. "We should be able to make it there and back."

They left his father in the hotel room, hard at work on his laptop, and rode to Laval, the island to the north of Montreal. Gil cried again when he saw the plot. Someone had planted a bush near the headstone. His mother had bought flowers, and she laid them across the grave.

She put a hand on Gil's shoulder. "I'll be in the car."

Gil waited until he heard her door shut. Then he crouched at the foot of the grave and dug a narrow hole in the damp earth with his fingers. He took off the silver band with its broken prongs, thrust it in as deep as it would go and covered the hole once again.

"It belongs here," he said, "with you. In Quebec." He wiped his fingers on his sweatpants and stood, breathing deeply. "You come from a beautiful land. I only wish . . . I only wish you were here to show me around." He couldn't say anything more.

His mother was quiet when he finally returned to the car. On the highway, he watched the passing suburban sprawl and cityscape—office buildings, warehouses, parking lots, malls, overpasses, billboards, apartment houses, a domed church on a hill. Yet there were no people—none visible anyway. Although every square inch had been touched by human hands, it felt empty. The loneliness overwhelmed him.

People began dotting the sidewalks when they reached downtown.

Mom spoke up. "We have time for lunch."

Gil thought for a moment. "I know a place."

The Apropoulis bustled as much as ever. Richeline winked at Gil. He gave her a sheepish smile. She led them to a booth.

"How about here?"

Mom scanned the plastic menu after they sat down.

"A Greek diner?" she whispered. "Are you sure?"

"Positive."

The food was as good as Gil remembered. Halfway through their meal, a large man walked in. Gil didn't recognize Maurice at first: he wore pressed slacks, a long-sleeve shirt and a tie, and his hair had been combed neatly about his face. But Maurice recognized Gil and waved. Gil waved back. He introduced him to his mother, who said hello—politely, but without warmth.

"The last time I saw Adèle," Maurice said, "she told me you went north."

Gil didn't want to talk about this. Not now.

But his mother had caught the name. "You know Adèle?"

"Yes. She's an old friend, I'm sorry to say."

Sorry? Gil stared in surprise.

Mom saw her opening. "Do you know how to find her?"

Maurice looked pained. "I wish I could. She disappeared a few days ago."

"Disappeared?" Gil asked.

"Her apartment is empty. No one knows where she went. I'm pretty sure she skipped town."

"What makes you say that?" Mom asked.

"She owed money to too many people," Maurice replied. "Including me."

So that was what they had argued over. A lot of things made sense to Gil now.

"Could she have gone back to where you grew up?" he asked.

"Marieville? Not likely. She doesn't have any family

there, not anymore. Her mother died a few years ago, and she never had a father."

Mom frowned. "Too bad."

"She took money from you, too?" Maurice asked.

"Almost all of it," Gil said.

"I am sorry. I tried to warn you."

"Yes. You did."

Maurice's eyes strayed to Gil's hand. "Did she steal the ring, too?"

Gil hesitated before answering. This was still too raw. "No." He swallowed. "It . . . it broke. . . ." He looked down at his plate.

"That is too bad," Maurice said. "I know it meant something to you."

"It's okay," Gil said, trying to recover. "It was just a stone set in poor silver."

He was parroting Miller's words. Sounding brave. Wouldn't do to break down in the middle of the lunch rush.

But somehow, the words did make him feel better. Even if only a little.

Mom seemed to have warmed to Maurice, now that she knew that he also held a grudge against Adèle. "Would you like to join us for lunch?" she asked.

"No. Thank you. I'm just picking up coffee. I teach a class in forty-five minutes."

"You're a professor?" she asked.

"Not yet. An assistant. I study engineering."

At least Adèle hadn't lied about that. Gil wished him luck with his class.

"And better luck to you," Maurice replied.

The check listed only Mom's chef's salad.

"There's a mistake," she told Gil.

"I don't think so. Just give them a big tip."

His mother stared at him, then nodded. When they went to pay the bill, Renée stepped out from behind the counter and gave Gil a motherly hug.

"He is a good boy, this one."

Gil blushed. Mom seemed surprised but nodded. Tony waved from the back.

"Come again!"

Gil started his senior year a week late. He didn't try out for any sports, but he resumed his daily runs up Overhang Rock. He spent afternoons working at a pharmacy, and every two weeks he mailed his paycheck to Hervé.

That fall was mild. The weather didn't turn cold until late in December, and even then, Gil could run with a sweatshirt. The knee he had beaten up so badly in Quebec had not only healed, it was stronger than ever.

Early one Saturday morning, he climbed to the top of the Rock, ready to greet the sun. His welcomes were muted now, but he figured someone should give the sunrise its due. A police cruiser was parked next to the war memorial. He ignored it. He stretched his arms up, extended his hands and brought them back down—to any observer, just a loosening stretch.

"Where's your partner?" the officer said.

She stood behind him. She must have been walking around the top. He turned around.

She held a paper coffee cup, her hands wrapped around the heat it generated.

"He's dead," Gil said.

"I'm sorry," the officer said. After an awkward moment she added, "Glad to see you're still running, though."

Gil gave her a small smile. "Thanks."

And as he headed back down the Rock, he realized how much her words had warmed him.

By the time he returned home, he was sweating despite the cold air. He felt alive. More alive than he had felt in months. In the shower, he vowed that someday he'd return to Quebec. He'd find a way to get a job. And he'd help Hervé float the white *chaloupe* in his barn.

Glossary

The French used in Quebec differs from the French spoken in France. It has its own accent, slang and turns of phrase. Some common words are different. I have translated the French words and phrases found in the novel as they would be understood by the Quebec residents using them. I have also included some English Canadian idioms.

absolument: Absolutely.

Ah non! Oh no!

américain: American.

anglo: Someone who speaks English. (A minority in Quebec.)

ben oui: Of course. (A contraction of *bien oui*.)

ben sûr: Definitely. (A contraction of *bien sûr*.)

bibliothèque: Library.

Bienvenu au Québec: Welcome to Quebec.

bon: Good.

bon Dieu: Good Lord ("good God").

bonjour: Hello.

Bouge pas! Don't move! (A contraction of *Ne bouge pas*.)

bûcheron: Lumberjack.

café: Coffee.

casse-croûte: Fast-food restaurant.

Ce n'est pas sérieux: It's not serious.

C'est qui, ça? Who is this?

chaloupe: An open boat, usually with benches, oar locks, a pointed prow and a square stern. It can range from very small, holding one or two people, to very large, capable of carrying heavy cargo and many people.

cimetières: Cemeteries.

cultivateur: Farmer.

décembre: December.

dépanneur: Convenience store.

De rien: You're welcome ("for nothing").

douze et cinquante: Twelve-fifty (twelve dollars and fifty cents).

draveur: Log driver. (A lumberjack who works on log drives over lakes and rivers in the spring.)

eh oui: Ah yes.

et: And.

étudiant: Student.

Fais 'tention! Pay attention!; Be careful! (A contraction of *Fais attention!*)

forgeron: Blacksmith.

frites: French fries.

grenat: Garnet.

Je peux t'aider: I can help you.

Je peux t'aider? Can I help you?

Je peux vous aider? Can I help you? (formal or plural).

jeune: Kid ("young").

Laurentides: Laurentian Mountains. A range in Quebec spanning northeast, to the north of the Ottawa and St. Lawrence Rivers. It is one of the oldest mountain ranges in the world.

le, la, l': The. (*Le* is masculine. *La* is feminine. *L'* is used before a vowel.)

librairie: Bookstore.

loonie: Coin worth one Canadian dollar. The coin has a loon on one side, giving it its name.

mais: But.

mais oui: But of course ("but yes").

mécanicien: Mechanic.

médecin: Doctor.

mémento: Keepsake; souvenir.

merci: Thank you.

monsieur: Sir.

non: No.

occupations régionales: Regional professions.

oui: Yes.

pardon: I'm sorry; excuse me.

peut-être: Maybe.

plus tard: Later.

poutine: A dish usually made of french fries, cheese curds and gravy. There are many variations.

privé: Private.

Québécois: Someone or something from Quebec.

Qu'est-ce que tu fais ici? What are you doing here?

Qu'est-c'est ça? What is this? (A contraction of *Qu'est-ce que c'est que cela?*)

Qui es-tu? Who are you?

quincaillerie: Hardware store.

scientifique: Scientific.

stade: Stadium.

toonie: Coin worth two Canadian dollars.

Tu reviens? Will you come back?

un, une: One; a/an. (*Un* is masculine. *Une* is feminine.)

un autre: Another one.

Université de Montréal: University of Montreal. It is the second-largest university in Canada and offers higher education in French.

Université Laval: Laval University. Located in Quebec City, it is the oldest university in Canada and was the first in North America to offer higher education in French.

Un peu. Juste un peu: A little. Only a little.

viens: Come along.

Voilà! There!

voyageur: A crew member on one of the large canoes that transported fur pelts across a wide swath of North America during the eighteenth and nineteenth centuries. Literally, "traveler." Most *voyageurs* were French Canadian.

voyons: Come on now ("look").

Author's Note and Acknowledgments

Thousands of years ago, a man named Gilgamesh ruled over Uruk, a Sumerian city-state in ancient Mesopotamia. Over time, legends about him grew, and more than three thousand years ago these were turned into an epic, written on twelve cuneiform tablets. Filled with gods, beasts, monsters, people from all walks of life, extraordinary deeds and wondrous settings, the epic told the very human story of a man who lost his best friend and had to confront his own mortality.

Gilgamesh, according to the tale, was a demigod and king. Enkidu was a man who lived with beasts. Yet they became inseparable. After many adventures they angered the gods, and Enkidu died. Gilgamesh, crazed by the loss of his beloved friend, went on a quest to secure immortality. He sought out Utnapishtim, who became immortal after he saved people and animals from a worldwide flood by building an ark. Though Gilgamesh tracked down Utnapishtim, he did not become immortal. He returned to Uruk defeated, but in the process, he became a better person and king.

Although Gil's story is not the same as Gilgamesh's, I kept to the epic's basic structure. I set Gil's quest in Quebec, a beautiful province with as much wilderness as Sumer ever had, filled with people as diverse as those in the Gilgamesh epic.

Although the settings in the novel are based on actual places, I have fictionalized them a great deal. Overhang Rock is similar to but distinctly different from East Rock in New Haven, Connecticut; I have moved buildings and paths around Mount Royal in Montreal; you will not find the Apropoulis nor Adèle's apartment in Montreal, although there are many buildings that might fit their description; and there is no town called Le Gros-Curé or lake called Lac de Couleurs in the Laurentians, though there are villages and lakes that resemble both.

I invented the legend of Antoine and Clotilde. However, garnet was once mined in the Laurentians, and for a long time lumber camps were ubiquitous.

I thank Gilbert Cholette of the Société d'Histoire de Chute aux Iroquois (Historical Society of Chute aux Iroquois) for the time he spent with me discussing the history of the Labelle region in Quebec, and for his detailed history of garnet mining in *L'exploitation minière à Labelle: Le grenat, Le graphite.* He introduced me to Madeleine Perreault-Cholette, author of *Labelle—La vallée de la Rouge—Tremblant,* which provides a delightful and useful history of the area. I would also like to thank the librarian at the Labelle public library who helped me find the historical information I needed, but whose name I am ashamed to say I did not write down.

Among my many early readers, I wish to thank Jed Backus and Sanna Stanley, who were willing to pick up the manuscript more than once and give me great feedback within a ridiculously short period of time. And I am immensely grateful to my daughters and husband, who read, gave feedback and set me straight on too many details and plot points to recount. (You could have said no. Really.)

My task was made immeasurably easier thanks to the advice and support I received from the talented members of Write Up Our Alley (Kate Duke, Deborah Freedman, Kay Kudlinski, M. W. Penn, Sanna Stanley, Leigh Ann Tyson and Cat Urbain), the folks at the Shoreline Society of Children's Book Writers and Illustrators, and my friends and family.

Special thanks go to my agent, Rachel Orr, whose guidance was invaluable; to the hardworking copy editors at Random House, who kept me on my toes; and to R. Schuyler Hooke, editor extraordinaire, who deserves several gold stars (not to mention a raise) for this one.

A. C. E. Bauer has been telling and writing stories since childhood. *Gil Marsh* is her first novel for young adults. Her previous middle-grade novels are *No Castles Here*, an ALA Rainbow List Selection, and *Come Fall*, a CCBC Choices Book. Born and raised in Montreal, she spends most of the year in New England and much of the summer on a lake in Quebec. To learn more about A. C. E. Bauer and her writing, visit her website at acebauer.com.